CHIL[illegible] O[illegible] EDGE

Stories of children around the world

Christine Leonard

in co-operation with Tear Fund

Scripture Union
130 City Road London EC1V 2NJ

By the same author:
Expecting the Impossible
Hidden in the Mist

First published 1995

ISBN 0 86201 934 6

British Library Cataloguing-in-Publication Data.
A catalogue record is available from the British Library.

Design by Tony Cantale Graphics.

Printed and bound in Great Britain
by Cox & Wyman Ltd, Reading, Berks.

CONTENTS

INTRODUCTION

Our world can appear complex, exciting, enormous and frightening all at the same time. But the world is also full of people, each with their own story to tell.

Stories can help us to understand what is going on in other countries. They can bring alive the exciting events. They can bring them down to a size we can understand. And they can help us to work out why these things have happened.

One day in Ethiopia I met a teenager named Tiekle. By the time I had heard her story my understanding was transformed. Before, I knew there were two million people facing starvation. After, of course there were still two million facing starvation, but for me one thing had changed. I now realised that every one was an individual, a person made by God. Each one had decisions to take, had their own hopes and fears, their own pain and joy.

Though the characters on the pages of this book are imaginary, they are based on situations which we at Tear Fund meet all the time. I am delighted that these stories offer a way into the real world that is the home of most of the world's children – a world which, all too often, we adults teach our children to ignore.

I hope that all the readers, and the hearers, of these stories will enjoy them; that the enjoyment will include understanding; that the understanding will lead to involvement.

Stephen Rand
Communications Director, Tear Fund

FACTFILE

BRAZIL

• To drive from the north to the south of Brazil takes over a week. Just that one country is nearly as large as the USA. Around half of all the people in South America live in Brazil – most of them in big towns rather than in the countryside. And half the people who live in Brazil are children.

• Most Brazilian families came originally from Europe or Africa or even Japan.

• São Paulo, one of the largest cities in the world, is one of the fastest growing too. More and more people come there from the countryside every day.

• About 17 million people live in São Paulo. Some are very rich, but many are really poor and live in terrible shanty towns called *favelas*. Hardly anyone there helps the poor people.

BRAZIL

May the Best Team Win!

I'm glad I picked the new boy for my team, thought Eliseu. He's ace at football! Just then, Antonio saw a gap, and passed the ball to Eliseu. As the team captain dodged around two defenders he could not help feeling proud of the way he controlled the ball. What an opportunity he and Antonio had set up!

Eliseu kicked the ball hard at the goal, but Celso sprang from nowhere and intercepted it. What a save! People cheered as the ball flew back to the centre forward, but then the whistle blew. End of the game and, despite everything, Celso's team had won again.

'You played brill today!' Eliseu congratulated young Celso, the football star of the village. He was just ten years old, and stocky, with the curly black hair of an African.

'I know!' Celso flashed his cheekiest grin, revealing a row of crooked white teeth. To think that he'd learnt most of what he knew in the couple of years he had been living here in Hope Village. Before that there had been no room for him to play football in the city. Anyway, it would have drawn unwelcome attention from the police, or the gang leaders, or the men with guns.

Celso had changed in other ways too. But then, in Hope Village, most people did. Especially those who, like Celso, had no mother or father.

'Remember the day you arrived here?' asked Eliseu.

'Not if I can help it!' came the answer, quick as a flash. 'I'd rather think about the day I leave!'

'What's wrong?' asked Antonio, concerned. He had been hanging around after the match because he liked Eliseu and had been wondering whether he dare invite him home. They were both the same age – twelve. But now he turned his attention to the younger boy, Celso. 'Don't you like it here?'

'Course I do! Only I've asked God for a family, you know, to foster me. That's what I want.' Then he dashed away.

'He's smelt dinner!' smiled Eliseu. 'D'you want to come round to my place later, Antonio? We need to discuss tactics or our team'll never win.'

Eliseu headed off to do his jobs for the evening – helping to milk the village cows and feed the sheep. Then it was time to make for the little red-roofed house with whitewashed walls which was his home. But during his family's evening meal only half of Eliseu's mind was on the rice and beans. The other half could not stop thinking about Celso.

Families from outside often came to foster those children in the village who had no parents of their own – but they took only the little ones, up to six years old, maybe. The cheeky young football star was four years too late. Everyone knew that, so why had he set his heart on a family of his own?

Sure, God answered prayers in the village. Otherwise Celso, like all the others, could never have been rescued two years earlier and brought here. His story was the same as that of many other children in the village. His parents had been so poor that they just could not manage. When he reached three years old they already had another toddler wanting food. They abandoned Celso to survive on the streets of São Paulo. In many ways he was lucky to have reached the age of ten – plenty died younger. And now he would be safe, in the village.

But still Eliseu worried. Suppose God didn't send a family for Celso? Would he go off into one of his tempers and smash the place up again, like he had in the old days? He'd been pretty tough for an eight year old – and never cared who he hit!

When Antonio came round they talked only about football, but later that evening, when the family gathered together to pray as usual, Eliseu mentioned Celso's dream of finding a family of his own.

'Poor lad! We'll certainly pray for him!' said Eliseu's father. 'And, if that's what he really wants, let's pray that he'll find a foster family. Though, if he does, everyone here will miss him!'

Some evenings people in Hope Village met to pray together in small groups. They also set a special building aside where at least one person would be praying at all times, day and night. Some of the grown-ups took it in turns. Marcos, the man who had started Hope Village, said that it only worked because God heard their prayers.

All of them, even the new boy, Antonio, knew the story of how, ten years before, Marcos had felt that God was telling him to build a village, right out here in the countryside, sixty kilometres from São Paulo. He had asked various families who loved Jesus to buy a little piece of the land where they would build their own house. Then, with the extra money from the sale, he had bought as much land again, so that they could grow food to eat and have plenty of space for other things too. As well as a school, they had a college, where older people could study the Bible.

As Eliseu had told Antonio, 'Marcos is ace. He makes sure that we always have somewhere to play football. And he even made the pond so that we could catch fish!'

The village was set in a fantastic place, with a little river and palm trees and plenty of wooded countryside to explore. Even school wasn't bad. The teachers were kind – they had to be, with a group of street children arriving every so often.

Most of those kids were really wild, even at the age of four. They'd had to learn to stick up for themselves on the streets and to grab anything they could. It took a while before they realised that the people in Hope Village were friendly and would share toys or food, or whatever was going.

The children who had been rescued from the streets of São Paulo lived in three special houses in the village, with special people to look after them. These included two psychologists – doctors who knew how the children's minds had been hurt by the terrible things which had happened to them, and helped them to get better.

Otherwise the children who had come from the streets went to school, played games and helped on the farm with the rest of the children, whose mothers and fathers had made their homes in the village.

Eliseu found it hard to imagine what it must have been like for Celso and the others – living on the streets of São Paulo, with no grown-ups to care for them. He had never even been to the big city.

After the prayer time that evening they all sat around drinking *cafezinho* – black coffee, very strong and sweet. Eliseu remembered that Antonio had lived in São Paulo with his family, until they had all moved to the village a few days ago. His father had come to study in the Bible College for a year or two, before going as a missionary to another country.

'What's it like in the city?' Eliseu asked, quietly.

Antonio paused for a moment. He was pleased that someone wanted information from him for once. Eliseu and the other children had been showing him who and what and how and why everything was in the village ever since he had arrived. But how could he even begin to describe the city?

'It's big.' He started, slowly at first. 'Utterly, gi-normously big – you can't begin to imagine. And modern. There are skyscrapers everywhere, they really do look like they have their tops in the clouds, sometimes. And there are shops and markets – you can buy anything – and loads of factories and traffic jams everywhere. They're always building new flyovers and things.'

'Good places to play football?' Eliseu interrupted. Antonio was now talking so fast that Eliseu found the words hard to follow.

'Oh yes – well, parks anyway. And all the stadia where the big teams play of course. I liked it where we lived.'

'And are there loads of children living on the streets?'

'I never really noticed them, until just before we came here. Dad took me to some places I'd never been to before. Dangerous sorts of places.'

'Were you scared?'

'Yep! We had to make sure we didn't look rich – we couldn't wear watches or good clothes or take cameras, in case we got mugged or knifed.'

'Boy!'

'And it was really poor and really dirty around there. And the skyscrapers, instead of being all shiny glass were kind of like dirty grey cliffs, shutting you in. And the walls were scribbled on and the alleyways smelt of wee. And there were yappy dogs, which ran out at us – I didn't like that. And a man kept following us, begging for money. He had yellow teeth and a horrible smile.' Antonio pulled a face.

'What about the children? How do they manage, all by themselves?' Eliseu wanted to know.

'I don't know! They don't have much – maybe a pair of pants and some flip-flops. The girls' hair looked like no-one had combed it for years!'

'But how do they get food and stuff?'

'We saw a few begging. One of them, his foot was all twisted round. Or they nick things, from people's pockets, or scrounge food from dustbins. And Dad said that they sell drugs for the gang leaders, who beat them up or kill them if they don't do it right. Or the police catch them because it's against the law to sell those kind of drugs. They're really bad for you. Some of the kids take the drugs and it makes them go all weird so that they don't know what they're doing.'

'Where do they sleep at night?' Eliseu asked.

'We saw some sleeping under a flyover or in odd corners – there was one boy in a cardboard box. They try to keep pretty much hidden, though. Dad said that sometimes they dodge down big sewers, like rats.'

'Yuk!'

'No one wants them. They scare tourists away because they're always stealing things. So people go round shooting them. Shopkeepers and people who run tourist places actually pay off-duty policemen, or gangs, to shoot street children – with guns!'

Eliseu had heard about that, but it still made him shiver. What kind of sick person would kill little children? He had nightmares sometimes about people shooting his friends.

To change the subject he asked, 'How do they choose the ones who come here?'

'Some friends of Marcos run "drop in" centres in different parts of the city,' explained Antonio. 'Dad took me to one. They dish out free food there – and the kids get to trust the adults who want to help them. After they've filled in all the papers and things, the children can come here if they want.

'Oh, and they even run a kind of school thing under one of the bridges. Some of the kids use the centre as a safe place to sleep. But I tell you, when they're awake – well, if you think the kids coming here are wild, you should see the types there! Talk about jumpy. And they swear and fight all the time, and smash things up and steal. I tell you, I was real scared about coming here and having to live with a crowd of kids like that!'

When Eliseu's mother came over to tell the boys that it was nearly bedtime, she overheard the last part of their conversation. 'Most of those kids don't even remember their parents,' she said. 'They've never known what it is to have someone who cares about them. So it's not surprising that they think that everyone's against them.'

She paused for a moment, then added, 'That's where Marcos was wise. He knew we couldn't bring them straight here from off the streets. They'd probably run away. But if they get used to dropping in to one of those centres and find that people there are kind and give them food, well, it's a start. You can't really help someone until they start to trust you.'

The next day Celso's football team won again. Eliseu grabbed Antonio for another discussion about tactics and they worked out a plan. Over the next few weeks Antonio proved his worth. Besides playing well himself, he helped Eliseu train some of the younger boys. Not only did each one's technique improve, but they learnt to work better as a team, passing the ball when they saw a gap, rather than keeping it all to themselves as they had done.

Before long they drew a game and then they won. That was worth celebrating!

As for Celso, he still talked, confidently, about the family which would be his one day. Sometimes, at night, Eliseu remembered to pray for him, though he had mixed feelings about the other team captain leaving. The opposition would be rubbish without Celso – no competition at all!

When it happened, it took them all by surprise – all except Celso. A lady, wearing a full skirt in bright shades of red and blue and green, came round the village one day. Her husband, in his smart suit, seemed quite dull by comparison.

He kept quiet, except to ask the occasional question. She laughed and joked and talked to all the children. Her husband was the one who stopped to watch that afternoon's football match, however.

Meanwhile, a group of small girls who had been playing on some swings nearby showed the lady around the rest of the village, each hanging onto her skirt or one of her arms, so that she seemed to move in a sea of dark-haired children.

But it turned out that she, as well as her husband, must have found a moment to speak to Celso. A week later he was brimming over with pride. 'I have a family!' he announced at the top of his voice as he ran at full speed around the village. Against all the odds, the couple had chosen, not one of the little girls, with their appealing dark brown eyes, but the much older Celso, with his crooked grin.

The day before he was to be fostered, the whole village

held a huge 'goodbye' party for him, with balloons and a special cake and everything. At the end, Marcos himself thanked God for Celso and prayed that he would be happy with his new family.

'Course I will!' said Celso. 'God gave them to me!'

The next morning his new mother arrived in a car to take him off to their *fazenda* – their big farm – where he would live from then on. Plenty of other children lived on the *fazenda*, because their parents worked there. So Celso would not be lonely. He promised to come back and visit Hope Village soon. Then, clutching his favourite ted, he climbed into the back seat of the car as though he had done it every day of his life.

Eliseu felt down for a moment as they waved goodbye to Celso. Then he made a difficult decision. He turned to Antonio.

'You're the top footballer now,' he said, 'and I'm the next best. I think it would be fairest if one of us switched. Are you going to captain Celso's old team, or shall I?'

THE SUDAN

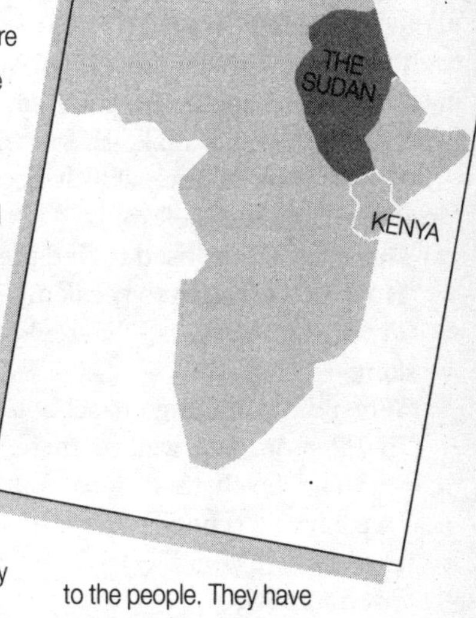

• The Sudan is the largest country in Africa.

• Most of the north is semi-desert. The people who live there are mainly Arabs who follow the Islamlc religion.

• The south is green, fertile and much wetter. African-type peoples live there.

• Since 1983, when the government tried to make the whole country follow Islamic laws, the southern Sudan People's Liberation Army has been fighting government troops who are based in the north.

• Homes have been destroyed and nearly all the men have been forced to fight. Farming is no longer possible and the war means that food cannot be sent to the people. They have nothing and can buy nothing. They are desperate.

• Tear Fund supports an organisation called ACROSS - Christians who try to help the Sudanese people. Their representatives met the 'lost boys' at Lokichokio.

THE SUDAN

The Lost Boys

Diya had arrived like all the other boys, walking. He carried everything he owned on his back, in a bundle of sticks wrapped in cloth.

Theresa, an Irish Red Cross worker, had been asked to find out more about the children. She had to talk as Diya worked, building a make-shift shelter out of his bundle of sticks. He showed such skill it became obvious that he had done it many times before.

Theresa was surprised to find that he spoke a little English.

'How did you learn to speak my language?' she asked.

'From our teachers,' he replied, not bothering to stop working.

'When did you last go to school?'

'In Pinyudo. We walked there. We heard people would help us and teach us lessons. But fighting came there and now we have no school.'

'How old are you, Diya?'

'I don't know.'

Theresa looked at him carefully. People of his tribe, the Dinkas, grew tall and Diya's legs, like his arms, were long and thin. Yet he could not be more than eleven. He would have been two when the war started.

'Where are your mother and father?' she asked.

Diya looked blank. 'Don't know.'

'Brothers and sisters?'

'Don't know.'

'Where did your family use to live?'

'In a village.' Diya swept his arm round in a gesture which could have meant anything. 'Far away, over there.'

'When did you last go to your own village, Diya?'

'Don't know.' He put the finishing touches to his shelter, tucking in plastic sheeting so that it would not blow away. Then he appeared to consider her question more seriously. 'I walked a long time. Then I found the refugee camp at Pinyudo – across in Ethiopia. Then I walked again,' he said.

Red Cross officials at the supply base of Lokichokio, just inside Kenya, were trying to work out what had been happening. The previous weekend, 21,000 people had streamed across the border from the Sudan and set up camp near their base. Of these, 16,000 were no ordinary refugees – that is families left with no home and no means of support because of the fighting. These 16,000 were all boys, ranging from teenagers down to six year olds.

For months there had been rumours about bands of boys, roaming about in southern Sudan, finding food where they could. The previous November 10,000 of them had turned up near a village called Gorkuo. Aid workers gave them some food, clothes and medicines. But within a couple of months the boys had to go, because fighting had started. Soon Gorkuo fell to the Northerners.

Some people thought the boys were a kind of secret army, kept ready by the Sudan People's Liberation Army guerilla fighters (the SPLA). Others thought that they were simply orphans – and certainly the Sudan had enough of those. But why all boys? And why so very many, all together? The more they found out, the stranger the story seemed.

After Gorkuo the boys turned up in Narus, still in Sudan but nearer the Kenyan base of Lokichokio. This time 5,000 adult refugees from the area around Gorkuo had come with the children. Relief workers tried to help – they even sent messages out as widely as they could into Southern Sudan, in case parents were looking for their lost boys, but very few turned up to find them.

As a site for a camp, Narus was terrible. First it flooded, then it dried out and the people had no drinking water. The boys grew increasingly afraid that the soldiers were coming. Suddenly they all left and crossed the lonely border into Kenya – coming even nearer to the supply base where Theresa worked.

Theresa considered all this information carefully before she continued to question Diya. 'You came from Narus?'

'Yes.'

'And before that?'

'Many places. When fighting came, we moved. We walked to find food.'

He turned and carefully placed his possessions inside the finished shelter – a battered saucepan and a small bundle of rags which Theresa thought must be his spare clothes. He wore some very tight, very small shorts and a torn shirt with a single button, which exposed the almost black skin of one of his shoulders. Like the rest of the children he had no shoes.

'I go now, to help the small ones,' he said and walked over to where a little boy was struggling to build his shelter. Theresa watched for a few minutes as Diya patiently showed the younger boy how to balance and tie the sticks.

Suddenly she realised one reason why this camp was like no other which she had ever visited. When people arrived in 'organised' refugee camps it could appear chaotic, as everybody jostled for whatever was going. But these boys just got on with things themselves. And instead of the usual quarrels, everywhere she could see the older boys helping the younger ones, with little fuss.

She moved on and found another boy, sitting in the dust. 'What is your name?' she asked, in the Dinka language.

'Peter,' he replied.

She went through the same questions, and received similar replies.

He looked younger, about seven years, Theresa reckoned, judging by the length of his thin legs. One of the many things which puzzled her was that, although these children looked all skin and bone, none of them showed signs of being dangerously malnourished or starving. She knew the danger signs. The tight, black curls on African heads would turn a reddish shade and their skin would develop strange blotches. Last of all, their stomachs would swell as though overfull – though in reality they might have eaten little for weeks.

But these children seemed healthy.

She tried some new questions on Peter. 'What did you eat, before you came here?'

'We found leaves and roots.'

'How did you find out the way to cook them?' she asked. Theresa knew that many were poisonous. Unless they were cooked at the right temperature for long enough, they could make you very ill or even kill you.

'The older boys help us. Sometimes they hunt an animal.'

'There are so many of you. How have you all kept safe?'

'Safe?' Peter shrugged. 'Many drowned crossing angry rivers after the rains. Wild animals took some – crocodiles, lions. Very many got sick and died. My best friend was shot by soldiers from another tribe.'

It was hot – 38 degrees Celsius. The flies were buzzing and Theresa felt confused. She moved over to a tree which would provide deeper shade, sat down and took out her note pad and pencil. She must try to make sense of some of the things which she had heard already, before interviewing any more children.

Something made her look up. A group of about twenty boys had gathered and appeared to be very interested in her.

'Hallo!' she said, in Dinka.

'Hallo,' one of them replied, in English. 'You have paper?'

'Yes,' she said, more puzzled than ever. If she had been sitting there eating she could have understood it, but why did they show such interest in her note pad?

Some of the boys were touching the paper, stroking it lovingly.

'We have no paper,' the first boy said, sadly.

'You want paper? Why?' asked Theresa.

'To teach writing,' said the boy, who looked older than the rest.

'Are you..? Are you a teacher?' she asked.

'He's our teacher!' replied a smaller boy, again in English.

'What's your name?' Theresa asked the 'teacher'. This was interesting. Reports from Gorkuo had said that older children called 'teachers' organised the boys, but she had not imagined that they would teach things like writing.

'Emmanuel,' the teenager replied. He looked from the note pad up to her face. 'You know algebra?'

Algebra? Theresa looked around at the huge numbers of people, all refugees, at the hot sun and the green trees and the dusty ground. Here she was, miles from any town, on the edge of a war zone, with hungry children who could not remember their mothers or fathers, or where they had come from. They had a real struggle from day to day, just to stay alive. And this boy of fifteen was asking her about a kind of mathematics which she had found particularly hard at secondary school and never used since. Algebra? She must be dreaming!

'You, um, you don't teach them algebra?' she asked.

'I do not understand much of it,' he said, sadly.

'What else do you teach?'

'Geography, English...'

Theresa could not believe her ears. Could this explain why many of the children spoke her language so well?

'But who taught *you* these things?' she asked, at last.

'Teachers at Pinyudo – and before that the older children,' Emmanuel replied.

Then he sent the others away and Theresa talked with him for a long time. She found out that the boys were divided into groups of about twenty and that each group had a teacher – an older boy who looked after them and taught them – not only school subjects, but how to build shelters and find food to survive. In return, she taught him what little algebra she could remember and he seemed amazingly grateful.

When they had finished he called his group of children together again. They're in for an algebra lesson, thought Theresa, with a smile.

'Good luck,' she said in Dinka to one of the returning boys. He looked surprised, but grinned at her.

'He's a Nuer,' explained Emmanuel.

A Nuer? Their tribe had never been friends with the Dinka people. But, as she looked around the camp that day, Theresa realised that Nuer boys did indeed live among the Dinkas who made up the majority. They all helped each other with no sign of the fighting which she would have expected. She knew that the different tribal groups within the rebel southern army fought each other as well as their northern enemy.

As she talked to more and more of the boys, Theresa began to build up a picture of at least part of the reason why they had left their homes and banded together on their long march round the countryside. Most of their homes had been destroyed, but, more than that, these boys did not want to fight. Far from being a secret 'army in waiting' for the SPLA, they had fled from the soldiers, who they believed might have forced them to fight. That was one reason why they made long treks across the barren countryside.

Theresa reported all this back to her bosses.

'Is that why there are no girls among them? Because only the boys feared being recruited by the SPLA?'

'Possibly. There were girls at Pinyudo, but they had adult relatives with them and I suppose they went off somewhere else,' Theresa replied.

'But are the boys safe from the SPLA here?' one of the others wanted to know. 'There's nothing to stop guerillas from swarming over the border and seizing them. Wouldn't it be better to move them further into Kenya?'

And so plans were made to transport the boys to a camp run by the United Nations High Commission for Refugees at Kakuma.

The next day was a Sunday. As Theresa walked around

the camp she heard music. A large group of boys was singing in the Dinka language. Some of them wore strange, white clothes which she had not seen the day before.

Theresa moved closer. They looked like choir robes – absurdly short and outgrown, but much less ragged than the clothes which she had seen yesterday. First algebra, then choir robes in this, of all places, she thought. Am I going mad?

The boys were singing in Dinka, and the words seemed to be a kind of hymn, or song, in praise of God. As she moved closer still and could hear individuals, she realised that some were singing the same tune, but in the Nuer language.

She sat around while one of the boys spoke and then they all sang again. She recognised the tune this time as one which might have been heard in a Sunday school before the war began. Again, she had the feeling that she must be dreaming.

Afterwards she spoke to some of the boys.

Yes, they had kept their choir robes from happier times. They carried them round in their bundles of sticks and, when they grew too ridiculously small, would pass them on to younger boys.

They called the boy who had spoken their 'pastor'. He could not have been to college or anything, Theresa realised.

'But he teaches us about God,' they said.

'Where did you learn that first song?' Theresa asked. 'I'd not heard it before and the words which I managed to understand were beautiful!'

'One of the boys made it up,' came the reply.

Theresa shook her head. Here were thousands of lost boys, with no parents or home, surviving against the odds in this war-torn place. They had dodged crocodile swamps in the rainy season and bullets all year round. They had looked after one another, despite the fact that some might have been considered enemies. And now she had found out that they had a real hunger – not just for food, but a hunger to learn. Some of them even had a hunger to find out more about God and to worship him, despite all the terrible things which must have happened to most of them.

When lorries came for the boys, Theresa felt sad to see them go. I know I'm being selfish, she thought, because they are bound for safety in Kakuma, but I have learnt so much from them during the few days I have known them and I should like to find out more. I do not understand them, but they have certainly shaken up my ideas. They are very special, those children.

HONDURAS

• Honduras is a hot, wet country which lies between North and South America. Though it is about half as big as the UK, only about five million people live there. Many of them cannot read or write, because there are not enough schools.

• The Miskito Indians live in a very different way from the rest of the people of Honduras and they speak a different language. They can be found in the northeast of the country in an area called Mosquitia, which is about the same size as Wales. It is full of wide rivers, swamps, lagoons and rain forest. You cannot go there by road – only by river, sea or air.

• Most of the rain forest which remains outside protected areas in Honduras will probably be cleared within the next ten to fifteen years.

• Every minute the world loses an area of rain forest the size of 100 football pitches. Half of the world's rain forests have disappeared since 1900, and the destruction is getting faster all the time.

• That is bad news for the people and animals who live there, but also for the rest of us. For example, rain forest plants give us half of all known medicines, yet many will become extinct in the next few years. Also the rain forests do a great job of using up carbon dioxide and making oxygen instead – just what the world needs.

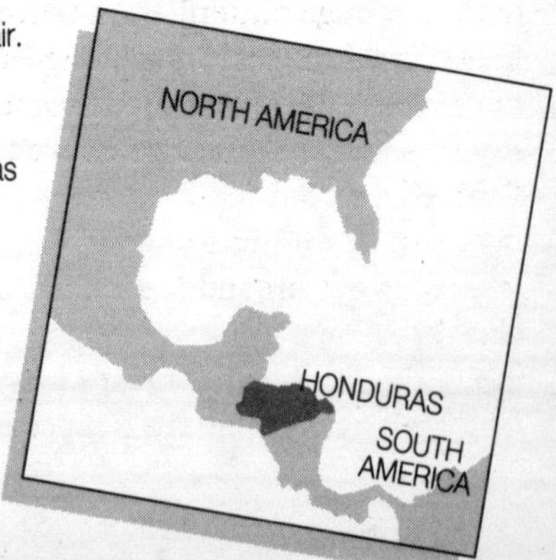

HONDURAS

Rain Forest Risk

The children stopped punting the canoe and let it drift slowly along the shallow water of the river's shore. Pedro always liked to look out for wildlife – especially for parrots and monkeys, though he often caught only tantalising glimpses of them through the thick jungly vegetation which grew right down to the river's edge.

Juanita simply enjoyed the lazy feel of the world slipping by as she looked up through layers of green leaves or, if they drifted further out into mid-stream, merely gazing at the intense blue of the sky. Green and blue made up the colours of her world – not forgetting brown, of course. Brown for the wide rivers and lagoons, and brown for the canoe, which had been hollowed by her father out of one huge log.

The trunks of the trees, however, looked grey like the mist when it rained. With her eye she followed the length of one giant of a tree from its top, high in the forest canopy. Its trunk was immense and straight, but near the forest floor it threw out great buttress roots to keep it steady.

There were other colours of course – the flittering yellows or reds of huge butterflies, the silver of the slippery fish which Pedro loved to catch, the orange and purple of fruits ripe for the picking. That reminded Juanita. They mustn't forget the reason why they had been allowed to take the canoe that day. Soon they would reach the trees which always bore especially tasty fruit at this time of year.

Juanita sat up and looked around. Although, to someone who lived outside the area, the river would have appeared much the same along most of its length, she knew that the fruit grew just around the next corner.

Pedro was already steering in that direction, but, when they rounded the bend, both brother and sister were surprised to see another canoe, similar to their own. On the bank were three children whom they did not recognise.

'Not from our village!' said Pedro. Though they had similar high cheekbones, big brown eyes and pale brown coloured skin to themselves, these were from another tribe – the Tawahka Indians. Pedro stopped punting to give himself time to see what was going on. The other children had tied their canoe to a branch and one of the boys had climbed the tree and was busy picking the fruit. It seemed especially plentiful this year.

Pedro's mouth watered. The other children spotted their canoe. They stared for a moment, then one of them, a boy a little older than Pedro's twelve years, waved and smiled.

'Hallo!' he called. 'Come for the berries?' He seemed friendly and the two children with him were also smiling and seemed pleased to see Pedro and Juanita.

Soon the canoes were lying side by side. Pedro started to climb the tree and was soon throwing the fruits down to Juanita and everyone was talking and laughing.

As they all worked the oldest boy said that his name was Henrique and that the other two, who seemed quiet and shy, were his brother and sister. Their father was one of the leaders of their village, evidently, which made them important people. Just as well they were so friendly, thought Pedro.

They came from a village upstream and so would have a difficult journey on the way back, whereas Pedro and Juanita would have an easy paddle with the current.

'You don't mind us sharing the berries, then?' asked Juanita, who often thought similar things at the same time as her older brother.

'Plenty for all,' smiled Henrique. 'For the moment!' But Juanita thought she saw a worried look cross his face.

'What's the matter?' she asked.

He replied with another question. 'Have men from

MOPAWI visited your village?'

'MOPAWI, what's that?' asked Pedro, puzzled.

'It's an organisaton which is trying to help people in our Mosquitia region to develop in a good way,' Henrique replied.

Pedro was still puzzled. 'I don't think anyone much comes to our village. It's up a side branch of this river which is too shallow for most boats.'

'Perhaps, then, my father should ask them to come,' was Henrique's surprising reply. He went on to explain that a couple of months before, two Miskitos from this organisation called MOPAWI had come to his village. They had arrived on the landing strip in a small aeroplane and met with Henrique's father and the other village leaders. They told grave news, which everyone found hard to believe at first.

'People from outside this region are wanting to move on to your land. You need some papers to prove that it belongs to you, or they will turn you out of here,' the two men had said.

Henrique's grandfather had been the hardest to convince. 'Papers? We don't need papers for our land!' he said. 'My grandfather lived and died in this village, and his grandfather before him and so on and so on, back to the dawn of time. This land is ours, I tell you, and no one can take it away from us!'

But the men from MOPAWI insisted that they knew differently and said that they had come to warn the village before it was too late. 'In the end they took my father and another man from the village for a ride in their plane.' Henrique laughed. 'No way would Grandfather set foot in it.'

Henrique admitted that he wondered if he would ever see his father again, but a few hours later all four returned and the two village men had tales to tell which sounded as strange as though they had visited another planet.

They had flown along the river and on either bank, for as far as their eyes could see, only blackened stumps showed where trees had once grown. Instead of the forest animals, cattle were grazing the thin grass. It had not seemed to be growing very well, perhaps because the hard hooves of the cattle constantly trampled it. It had begun to rain heavily and it seemed that much of the soil was being washed into the river, turning it a deeper shade of yellowish brown.

The men from the plane had explained how the Indians who used to live in those parts had now fled. The strangers came from another part of Honduras and had a hard time farming there. So they had got special papers which said that the forest land belonged to them.

The Tawahka Indians, who had lived in that part of the forest for as long as anyone could remember, had no papers. As far as they knew, *they* owned the land, but no one had ever tried to take it off them before. Because the Tawahkas had no way of proving that the land was theirs, the strangers simply took it. They had guns to back them up.

The Tawahkas could no longer hunt or gather food in the forest, since all the forest had gone. They could not live on fish from the river alone, and they needed leaves and branches to make or repair their homes. They also needed fibre from forest creepers to tie the structures together. They had no choice but to move on to try to find new homes in another place, but this made them very sad, for, without the forest, they knew that their way of life would die out.

Henrique's father knew that if what the men from MOPAWI had said was true – that Indians were being pushed off their land like this – soon there would be no more 'spare' forest left. And the Tawahkas, well, would just not be Tawahkas without their forest.

Back in the village, Henrique's father had called everyone together. The men from MOPAWI explained that they needed to have something written down to show that they owned the land around the village, otherwise more cattle farmers might come and try to take it off them too.

'At first, we didn't know whether to trust the two men,'

said Henrique. 'They left in their plane, but when they came back, six days later, my father asked them to help the village get the pieces of paper which would prove that we owned the land.'

'And what happened?' asked Pedro.

'They have worked hard for us,' Henrique said. 'No one has tried to take our land ... yet. But if they do, I think that they will not find it so easy, now.'

By this time, the children had finished picking all the berries which they could reach. Henrique's words had so worried Pedro and Juanita, that they decided to paddle back to their own village as quickly as possible to tell their father about the new danger.

'Could we bring some of the people from our village to visit yours?' Pedro asked. 'I'm not sure that the grown-ups will believe us, you see.'

'Of course,' said Henrique. 'You will find it about an hour from here, on this bank.'

They waved goodbye and then Pedro skillfully manoeuvred the canoe out into the main stream of the river.

Pedro and Juanita arrived back at their own village sweating and out of breath, because they had paddled hard. Some of their little brothers and sisters, who had not been allowed on the canoeing trip, came racing down to the riverside, and squealed with delight when they saw the berries. They all helped to carry the load back to their house. It was perched high on stilts, to keep it dry during the frequent downpours, when the land turned to mud. But, since it had not rained today, Mother was cooking on a fire outside, preparing rice and beans for the evening meal.

For once, however, Pedro and Juanita were less interested in food than in finding their father. He listened patiently, only saying from time to time, 'Slow down!' And he agreed to talk to the leaders of the village about the worrying news, after they had all eaten their meal.

The leaders looked concerned, as Father explained the

children's story. 'But this land is a forest reserve, set aside for the plants and animals and for us Indians,' one of them said. 'No one is allowed to cut down trees, or to burn them. The government of Honduras would stop them.'

'Yet these people said that the forest was finished twenty five kilometres from here,' said Father. 'Should we not go and find out more from the Tawahka village?'

And so it came about that a canoe-load of men from the village went to visit Henrique's father in his village. He was able to answer many of their questions. Yes, the land for many hour's canoeing all around did belong to the forest reserve and he agreed that it should have been protected by the government of Honduras. Yet only three men were paid to protect all that vast area. They tried their best, yet what could they do?

Once the trees had gone, the soil in which they had grown soon disappeared. Even if people tried to plant new ones they would not survive. On the other hand, the timber and the meat from the cattle could be sold to the USA, not only making the farmers rich, but bringing in money which the country of Honduras really needed.

Another question which had worried the men of Pedro's village was why the men from MOPAWI had bothered to come in a plane to help a few poor Indians. Henrique's father said that he had wondered about that at first, too. But the men had said that they cared about the forest and about the Indians, who had lived off it for so long without destroying it.

They had said that the Indians understood the forest. They knew how to farm the land in a way that did not damage the trees, and were able to produce crops which they could both eat and sell. The men from MOPAWI said that other people in Honduras needed to learn from the Indians. They and the forest were far more important than beefburgers – which was how the cattle would end up!

In the end, everyone in the village had grown to like and to trust the men from MOPAWI and were very grateful for their help. 'No one else has ever bothered to stick up for us!' Henrique's father said.

Pedro and Juanita waited eagerly for their father and the leaders to return. When they did, the whole village gathered together in the little wooden church building. Most of the Miskito people had become Christians around a hundred years before, when some Moravian missionaries had come to tell them about Jesus.

'We have asked for the men from MOPAWI to visit us too,' explained one of the leaders. 'We have learnt that they also are Christians and that they care about us and about the forest. They believe that God made everything and that he also cares. That is why they are trying to warn us. So we must thank God and thank them. And, if they are able to help us against this danger, then we must also thank Pedro and Juanita, here – and their good friends in the village down the river.'

The two children looked at each other and both felt shy suddenly, so that they bent their heads and looked at the ground instead. Pedro saw an ant scurrying across a tree root, Juanita noticed a beautiful mauve orchid. Both of them were thinking exactly the same thing again.

Pedro spoke so quietly that only his sister heard him. 'Our land is a good land,' he said. 'No way are we going to lose it!

FACTFILE

THE PHILIPPINES

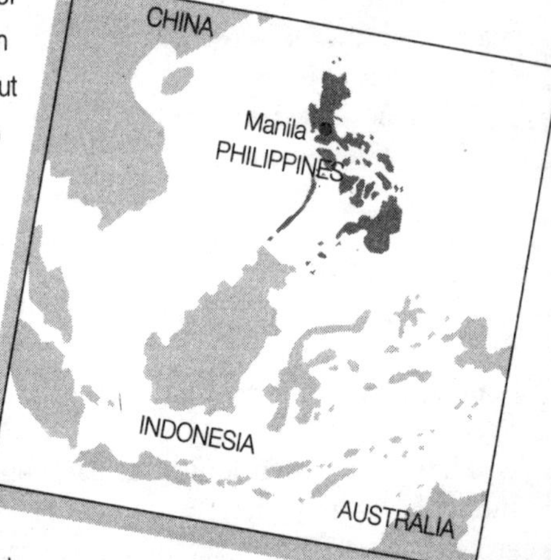

• The country is made up of 7,107 islands, but less than half have names. Only about 1000 have people living on them – the rest are deserted apart from birds and animals.

• The islands lie near the equator in the hottest region of the world, known as the tropics. Rain forests used to cover them, but most have been cut down now.

• A shallow sea separates most of the islands, but to the east is one of the deepest parts of the ocean. It is 10,539 metres to the sea bed – deeper than Mount Everest is high!

• About 64 million people live in the Philippines - about eight million more than in Great Britain – and both have about the same amount of land.

• In 1986 they found that the president's wife had 2,700 pairs of shoes and washed in a basin made of gold, while many people in the country which President Marcos ruled were desperately poor.

THE PHILIPPINES

Home is a Dump!

Rothie wriggled in his seat. The fat lady who was squashing him against the side of the bus gave him a hard look. So what, he thought? His legs had been well pecked by her chickens, which were jammed in a basket underneath them both.

It seemed to Rothie as though they had been bumping up and down in this hot, smelly bus for ever. Just then his mother glanced round and gave him one of her smiles. That made him feel better, until he caught sight of her face reflected in the window. Now that she thought no one was looking at her she seemed tired and sad. Why did they have to leave home? He hadn't imagined it would be like this.

Rothie thought back to that morning when he and his brothers and sisters had said goodbye to their friends at the village where they had all been born. He wasn't supposed to cry now that he was eleven. But, no matter how fast he blinked, he hadn't been able to stop his nose and eyes running, so he had to pretend that he had lost something important beneath the raised floor of their old house.

He had always taken the village for granted, and only realised now what a good place it was to live. Palm trees shaded you from the hot sun. A huge sandy beach made a really decent place to play. The sea, just a few metres from their house of cool bamboo and palm thatch, was safe and shallow – and he loved to swim in it all the year round.

It took Rothie by surprise that he was thinking this way. He had been the one who had longed to go to the big city. Mum and Dad had certainly not wanted to, nor had little Berta. Even his big, teenage brother Lario seemed uncertain, but then he had always enjoyed helping Dad with the fishing.

Poor Lario had been the most upset when the typhoon smashed up their boat – and most of the other boats in San Marcos as well.

It was only a few weeks ago when Mum and Dad had called the family together.

'We can't last like this much longer, we'll starve!' Dad had said.

He had explained the Big Plan then – how they must leave the village and travel to the big city – to Manila, the capital of the Philippines.

'They say that you can find work there. Not fishing, but other work. And so we shall make a new start, all of us.'

Rothie fell asleep in the end, as the bus bumped on and on past endless rice fields gleaming in the sun.

When he woke, night had fallen and the view through the windows was unlike anything that he had seen before. Lights shone everywhere. They beamed from shops and houses, and from the brightly decorated 'jeepney' taxis which surrounded them in one huge, noisy traffic jam. But most amazing of all, Rothie thought, were lights which spelt words, words which flashed in different colours. 'Coca Cola,' said one, 'Sprite' another, while a third advertised 'Wimpy Burgers'.

What a place, thought Rothie, wide awake and excited by now. He knew they would like it here, but no one had told him that Manila was full of such amazing food and drink. Beats boring old fish and rice, he decided, his mouth watering.

Then the bus stopped and everyone still left on it got off. Dad checked that the family had collected all the things which they had been carrying and they started to walk down the road together.

'Where are we going?' Rothie asked, but his father did not seem to know. He stopped at one tatty-looking hotel, but the prices it charged were far too expensive for the family to stay the night.

Little Berta complained of sore feet. In the end Mum said

that they had to stop somewhere and so they huddled in a shop doorway.

It rained later that night and most of Rothie's clothes felt wet by morning. In the daylight the streets looked messy.

'Can't you find us anywhere to live, Dad?' Rothie asked, crossly. At least they had been able to buy some hot rice at a road-side stall, but he knew that their money would not last for long, unless some of them could find work soon.

Dad and Lario decided to go in separate directions to look for work, but by the time they all met up again a few hours later, they already knew that it was hopeless. The streets were crowded with people. And it seemed that most of those people were also looking for a job – any job.

But they must live somewhere, thought Rothie. They were queueing at another stall to buy some more hot rice. Rothie was fidgeting around as usual and suddenly realised that he was standing on someone's toe. He looked round, to see a boy, maybe a couple of years older than himself.

'Sorry!' said Rothie.

The teenager had looked annoyed, but now he smiled. 'No problem! What's your name, kid?'

'Rothie.'

'Mine's Johnny.'

Johnny liked to talk, and Rothie soon found out that he lived 'quite near' and that he had arrived in Manila from the country, just like them, about a year ago.

'I came with my mum, but she died soon after, so I live with some friends. Maybe you could live around there too.'

By now Dad and Lario had gone off again, promising to meet the rest of them by a bridge over the River Pasig which flowed, wide and muddy, right through the city.

It turned out that Johnny lived, not in a house, but in a shack, about two metres by three with a roof made out of old bits of iron. Johnny tapped the thin wood of one of its walls.

'I found this old packing case myself,' he said, with pride. 'We'll try and grab you something and maybe you could live over there.' He pointed across a huge area full of shacks similar to his own.

'Doesn't this land belong to anyone?' asked Mum.

Johnny shrugged. 'When it rains you'll find there's water everywhere. The railway line's just over there and the town's rubbish tip is on the other side.' That would explain the smell, Rothie thought, but Johnny was continuing.

'I don't think anyone rich or important would want this land, even if they did own it. But there might be room for you!' He began picking his way between the shacks. Rubbish lay underfoot, everywhere – wet rubbish, and it smelt too.

'No toilets, and no drains, that's why!' grinned Johnny, when he saw little Berta holding her nose.

'Electricity though,' said Mum, pointing to a TV aerial.

'We get it from the cables up there!' said Johnny. 'But it's dangerous, tapping into the mains – and some of the people round here are dangerous too. Three were killed last week. There are gangs with guns and knives.'

That surprised Rothie. He had thought how neat and tidy everyone looked, despite the fact that they had no proper place to wash or clean their clothes. They seemed ordinary and nice, just like his friends in the village back home.

'Most people here are really kind,' explained Johnny, 'but you have to watch out for the bad ones.'

The smell seemed to be getting worse and soon Rothie realised why. Above the shacks, high above, towered a great mountain of rubbish. Gulls wheeled overhead, while on the ground great yellow digger trucks dumped yet more rubbish on the pile. At this distance the people who scurried about looked as tiny as insects.

'Whatever are they doing?' gasped Mum. Two or three seemed in danger of being crushed beneath the caterpillar tracks of the huge trucks.

'Want a house? Want a job?' said Johnny, mysteriously. 'Come and see!'

Rothie felt a bad mood coming on. The smell made him

feel sick and he didn't understand what Johnny was talking about, or why he was making them begin to climb up, over the mountain of rubbish, which squelched black and rotting beneath their feet.

Suddenly Rothie stopped and refused to go on.

'Look, it's on fire!' he said, pointing to thick white smoke which emerged from the tip a few feet away from where they were standing.

'Got it in one!' said Johnny. 'They say it burns away, day and night, under the surface. All that stuff rotting makes it get hot.' He laughed at their worried faces. 'It's never gone up in flames yet, though,' he said and continued to pick his way upwards until they came to a flatter place where the great yellow trucks drove to and fro.

'Who are all these people?' asked Mum. Old men and young boys were turning over the rubbish with sticks. Women were there too. Each carried a bag or a basket slung over their back in which, from time to time, they would carefully place some object which they had found.

A couple of tiny children with dirty hands were playing near their mothers, sometimes putting pieces of rubbish into their own mouths. Rothie was not surprised that their faces looked raw with sores. But the older children, with their big dark eyes, had beautiful skin. They look just like my friends from the village, he thought. A little thinner, maybe, but they laugh just the same.

According to Johnny, around 4,000 people worked this rubbish dump. 'Most of them live down in the shacks, like me,' he said. 'We earn our living by finding things which other people have chucked out. Then someone else sells it for us. This is the day shift. Different people work it at night.'

'Yuk!' said Rothie, but Johnny had seen something and was already hurrying off towards a truck which had just arrived. He pounced on a battered packing case almost before it hit the ground.

'Walls already!' he yelled, above the noise of the engine.

They found no metal sheeting that day, but by the time they had to meet the others by the bridge they had collected some polythene which Johnny said would do as a roof for now. They staggered down from the dump and laid it all in a pile, which Johnny said he would guard. Berta stayed with him, because her feet hurt.

Dad and Lario met the others by the bridge, but they had still not found work or anywhere to live, so the whole family came back to help build the shack. Johnny had scrounged some nails from somewhere. They cut holes in the wood for the windows and door and weighed the roof of polythene down with stones. The floor was just the mud on the ground. That night, when a rat paid a visit to the shack and brushed past his face, Rothie decided that he preferred sleeping in a shop doorway. But Mum insisted that at least this was a start – and it was their own.

The next day, Johnny helped them all to find bags and sticks and they set to work up on the rubbish dump, picking out anything which could be sold as scrap. Other people helped them too, showing them the kind of things to look for. Used paper, bottles and cans could all be sold. One old lady told Mum about a school nearby. Perhaps Berta could go there. Mum set out to find it.

At eleven, Rothie was too old for free school. He felt proud to be able to help earn money for the family, though by the end of the first day his muscles were stiff with bending over as he sorted through the rubbish.

Finally Johnny took the family to see a man who paid them a little money for some of the things which they had collected. At least they would eat better tonight – maybe they could even buy some *adobo* from the *carinderia* – the snack shop. This was Rothie's favourite dish – chicken and pork cooked in a special sauce.

As they made their way back to the shack, Rothie wondered how they would ever get clean. 'Even if I went back to San Marcos and swam in the sea ten times,' he said, 'I think I would still feel dirty!'

Back at the shack, Mum began squashing cockroaches. She had found seven, but cheered up a little when Johnny came running into the shack carrying a basin.

'For washing clothes!' he said, 'and here's a straw broom for sweeping up in the morning.'

'You're so good to us, Johnny,' said Mum. 'Thank you!'

'People were good to me when I first came,' he replied. 'I felt so lost and so homesick for my island of Negros.' His eyes went all dreamy. 'You know, the mountains there are not made of rubbish. They have white clouds at the top and thick green forests on their sides. There are waterfalls and hot springs and coral reefs, but ... no work, no money. You can't eat a beautiful place and I didn't want to die – so, I decided to make the best of things here. It's not so bad.'

That night, before he went to sleep, Rothie stepped out into the alleyway and looked up at the mountain of rubbish. He could see the smoke in the lights which moved over it – lights from the trucks and from the rubbish-pickers on night shift, and lights from the huge city all around. Nine million people lived there, they said.

And then he saw something which he had not noticed by day. Against the artificial lights and the white, drifting smoke, the shape of a little cross showed blackly. Then he remembered that Johnny had said something about a church. Rothie didn't like church much. Yet, Johnny had talked about some man in charge of a church round there, who lived in a shack himself and helped the people whenever he could. Johnny made him sound really kind.

That started Rothie thinking. Perhaps there was good in the world after all. Perhaps he and his family would earn enough money so that he could study some more and get a better job. Then they would all be able to find somewhere less smelly to live! He turned back into the shack, flicked away the mosquitoes and settled down for the night.

BURKINA FASO

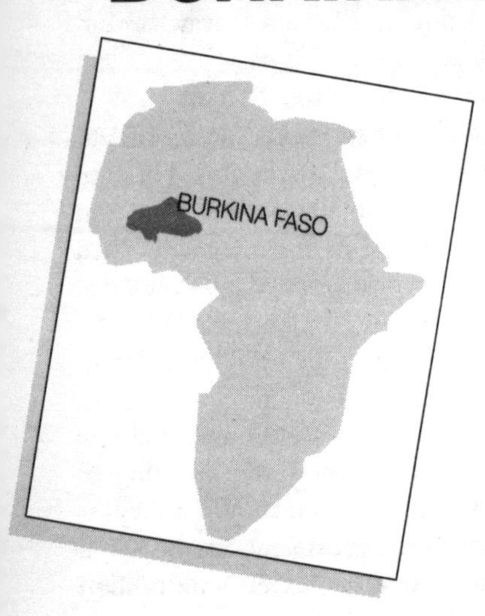

• The country of Burkina Faso in West Africa is a bit bigger than the UK, but the UK has over six times as many people.

• It is one of the poorest countries in the world. There is little work other than farming.

• The Sahara desert has moved 350 kilometres further into Burkina Faso during the past twenty years. It used to rain heavily during part of each year, but since 1968 it has not rained nearly so much. People suggest different reasons why this should be – the world is heating up, the forests are being cut down – but no one really knows. About one fifth of the earth's land is in danger of turning into desert before long – and nothing will grow there.

• A person can live for only three days without water. Many people who live in Burkina Faso have to walk for several kilometres to find clean water.

• In Burkino Faso, as in other African countries, many women spend around four hours a day carrying water to their homes. They balance it on their heads in containers which, when full, weigh 20-30 kilos. When water is difficult to find, people cannot wash things properly and infections of the skin and eyes spread more easily.

BURKINA FASO

Desert-busters

'Hey! Come back!' Out of the corner of his eye, René caught a glimpse of one of his family's chickens, disappearing behind a hut. He made a running dive for it. He had thought he had shut them all up for the night, but he mustn't have counted them properly, he realised – and this one had almost escaped. It squawked and wriggled now in his strong dark hands.

'In you go with the others,' he said, counting more carefully this time. He found it difficult to concentrate on his chores that evening. The whole village was almost dancing with excitement over the two men they were expecting to come the very next day. After waiting so long, could it be possible that something might happen at last? René hardly dared hope. He tried not to think about it as he led the floppy-eared goats into their hut – an easy job, now that only two were left.

One good thing about having no grain – he could forget guarding the store. No more hoicking himself up over the stilts it stood on. No need to wiggle in through its secret entrance and check the levels to make sure that no people, or rats, had stolen any.

René came back to the centre of the circle of huts and let his eyes run around their curved mud walls. The shape of their roofs – a cone, with the straw tied together at the top – showed clearly against the evening sky.

Six o'clock, and it was nearly dark. There, as usual, was Grandfather, sitting in the firelight, with the other children already gathered around him. He was waiting for René to arrive before he began the evening's story.

The custom had begun when Mother had tired of the little ones pulling at her skirts while she prepared the evening meal over the open fire. Now that they had only berries to eat – berries which took ages to cook – René did not know if the stories had become more or less important, only that he always loved listening to Grandfather.

Little Pinoaga was already clamouring for his favourite story. 'Tell us about when you were a boy, Grandfather. Tell us about the lions in the big forest!'

Grandfather laughed his deep laugh. 'What, again, young one?' And then he paused and seemed to think. 'Well, yes, perhaps tonight of all nights, that would be the best story, for it concerns a time when we had water and when the land was green. May it be so again!'

Oh, yes, thought René, watching his mother stirring the cooking pot. Just as well she prepared the berries so carefully – another family who only boiled theirs twice had terrible stomach aches and became really ill. René wished they had other food, though. They had walked for hours and hours to collect those berries, and they would still taste disgusting!

Grandfather had already started the story. 'Long ago,' he said, in a voice which seemed to come up from deep in his stomach to fill the night air, 'long ago, when my hair was not white, but black, and I was about as old as you are now, Pinoaga, trees grew in this place. Not just one or two, but a whole forest. Thick, it was, and hard to walk through, except on certain paths which we came to know.

'We farmed in the forest. The men would take their machetes – their big knives – and cut down trees and bushes to make a clearing. Then, while the grown-ups built the huts, we children would help scrape at the ground and plant some seeds. We would water them each day and soon the crops would begin to grow.

'We would stay in one place for two or three years, until the soil tired of growing food for us and then we would all move to another place. Often we found a clearing which my grandfather had made, thirty or so years before. The forest had planted itself there once more, of course, but young trees were only as tall as a man and easy to cut down.

'My parents usually remembered the place, and knew the paths through the forest, but we children didn't – and that was how we were nearly caught by lions!'

The story continued, as Grandfather told how he and his childhood friends had managed to escape from the lions. One of the children had spotted an opening in the trunk of one of the great trees and they all managed to squeeze inside. Even that might not have saved them, but Grandfather remembered that he was carrying a small animal which he had found dead in a trap earlier that morning. Before he dived inside the tree he threw it as hard as he could into the forest and the lions ran after it. Even so, none of them had dared come out of the tree for quite a while.

René found himself wishing, as always, that lions lived here now – and monkeys and parrots, and that grass grew tall enough to hide elephants. Those were the kinds of things which Grandfather had loved when he was a boy.

He said that rivers used to flow for much of the year – and that the villages always had water in their wells, even in the dry months from November to April. For, even when Grandfather was a boy, the rain only fell during certain months of the year.

'But what happened to all the trees?' René asked, as Grandfather finished the story. He knew only too well how far they had to walk over bare rock and yellowish dust before they found any tree with a green leaf or two, let alone nuts or berries. They passed a number of dead tree stumps on the way, but still René found it hard to imagine anything like a forest.

'People burnt them for firewood,' came the reply. 'And you know, though trees grew again on the land which we had farmed, they were never as big and strong. And the soil began to blow away in places where no tree roots held it together and no leaves fell to help keep it good. Nothing much will grow on rock or sand.'

Not even grass any more, thought René, except in a few places.

Just then Mother called out, 'Dinner time!'

René worried most about his mother. She looked so tired with all the extra work. She carried her head stiffly and sometimes he saw her wince with pain. She had to walk for miles and miles, now that their own well had only mud in the bottom of it. And she had hurt her neck, carrying the heavy pots full of water back to the village on her head.

Before they ate, Grandfather prayed, thanking God for the food as usual. He also prayed that the men coming the next day would be able to do something for the village. 'Powerful God, we know that you will not abandon us, your children,' he prayed. 'Your Bible says that streams of water will flow through the desert and that the burning sand will become a lake. May these men who are coming to our village help us to find the water which will bring new life to our homes and land – water which will make our hearts glad!'

The next morning, René woke early, and remembered at once why he felt excited. Water! The village would surely die without it. Or they would have to leave, as some of the older teenage boys had done already, to try their luck in Ouagadougou, the capital of Burkina Faso. Some had even travelled to a far-away country called the Ivory Coast.

But if the men coming today could somehow help them find water, he and his family and friends could stay in the village and grow their crops and feed their animals again. Then they could all eat properly and his mother would not have to spend every minute working so hard.

René and the other children finished their chores without being told and were all ready by the time the two men arrived in their Land Rover. Though it was still early, a fierce sun shone out of a cloudless blue sky.

After exchanging many greetings, they all sat down on the ground, crowding into any little bit of shade which they could find. One of the men, Monsieur Flanc, started to explain how things might improve.

'The problem is that, when the rains do come, most of the water just runs away.' Monsieur Flanc came from Burkina Faso, spoke their language, and looked like the men of the village, except that he wore a safari suit, instead of old, worn shorts.

He explained various ways in which they could catch the water which fell in heavy downpours from time to time during the rainy season. For example, over there (he pointed to where the valley narrowed) they could make a small dam from stones and earth. The water would run off the hills, when it did rain, and form a little lake behind the dam. With luck, its water would last well into the dry months.

Later, maybe, they could plant some trees on the lake's shores. Trees would shade their crops from the burning sun and keep the soil from blowing away.

Monsieur Flanc said that, if they would all come with him up a small hill near the village, he would show them how to make something even simpler.

He asked for a volunteer to help him carry something long and awkward. René arrived at the Land Rover before any of the others and so he helped Monsieur Flanc and the other visitor to lift a long pipe out of the back. It felt quite heavy.

René could see right through the pipe and he noticed that it was three quarters full of water, which slopped about as they walked along. None dripped out, though, for the ends of the pipe were well sealed.

When they had climbed half-way up the hill, Monsieur Flanc asked them to put the pipe on the ground. Then he came to René's end and helped him shuffle the pipe up the hill a few centimetres – and then a few more.

'See how the water in the pipe is level now?' he said. 'We need to mark carefully the line of this pipe. Then, if we arrange stones along the line, they will stop the rain running away downhill so fast.'

'But won't the water run through the stones?' René asked.

'Yes, but some of it will have time to soak in. And also, the stones will trap some of the earth which the rain would otherwise wash away. And that will trap more water and so on. In the end there will be plenty of wet soil and your crops will love it!'

Everyone else had run for stones, even little Pinoaga. Once the line had been marked carefully, Monsieur Flanc showed them how to move the pipe a little further round the hill.

'Put your end down and make it level again, René,' said Monsieur Flanc. 'Well done! Now bring more stones – and if we keep on doing that we shall have a line which goes right round the hill, all at the same level – on what we call a "contour line". And the line of stones we call a "diguette".'

He suggested that they should build many such lines at different levels all down the hillside. He encouraged them by saying that he knew of a number of villages which had found that, in this way, they could grow many more crops.

Monsieur Flanc smiled as he looked around him at the parched earth and the dry skeletons of trees. 'You may not think that you have much around here, but at least you have many, many stones!' Everyone laughed.

Both of the schemes would be hard work and everyone in the village would have to help. René glanced around. They all seemed keen to start. The village elders said that they would consult about the best places for the dam and diguettes and then they would begin building straight away.

'If you make these things, you know that you will have to look after them as well?' Monsieur Flanc said.

'We will!' said the village chief. Of course they would.

'But what about the flat land over there?' asked Grandfather.

'Well,' replied Monsieur Flanc, 'you know how, when the top of the earth is baked hard by the sun, the rain cannot soak in, even where the ground is flat? If you dig little troughs they will trap rainwater for long enough to give it a chance to seep down into the hard crust of the soil. If you plant the crops in those troughs, they should grow.'

'Now, about water for drinking!' It was the other visitor's turn to speak and everyone listened intently. 'I will take some measurements and decide if a deeper well would work here.' He said that it would cost money, but he did have a fund given by Christians in richer countries for just such things. René hoped that they could have one, because otherwise they would have to wait for the next rains before anything changed.

It took time before the well was dug and working. But the first time they lowered the bucket and brought it up full of good, clean water, they had such a party! René had never known anything quite like it before. The dancing and drumming continued for most of the night.

Next day, René's smallest sister Josephine trotted back and forth with a small container, carrying water from the well – which showed how close they had built it to the village! It took longer for the diguettes to start working, of course, and longer still for the lake to begin to fill.

But, by the next dry season, green shoots showed through the earth and this time they did not shrivel up in the hot sun. They grew into fine crops of millet and maize. René began to hear a familiar sound which he had missed in the village ever since the grain stores ran out. The women had once again taken up their big sticks, shiny with use, to pound the grain in wooden containers.

People in the village sang at their work. Even Mother laughed and had time to tell stories of her own around the fire of an evening. Afterwards, when René fell asleep, he dreamt of lakes and grasslands, of lions and elephants and forests and many, many adventures. Best of all, when he woke, he could still almost dare hope that, perhaps ... one day, his dreams might come true!

INDONESIA

• Indonesia has the fifth largest population of any country in the world. It is made up of thousands of islands – 13,600 to be precise, though over half have no people on them.

• It has 167 active volcanoes and lies in a region which has lots of earthquakes. If these happen at sea, they produce huge *tsunamis* (sometimes called tidal waves) which travel at about 700 kilometres per hour, destroying most things in their path.

• In 1883 the whole island-volcano of Krakatoa exploded. The *tsunami* made by the explosion killed 36,000 Indonesians.

• Flores Island has just over a million people, unexplored jungle full of crocodiles, and tribes which still hunt with blow guns.

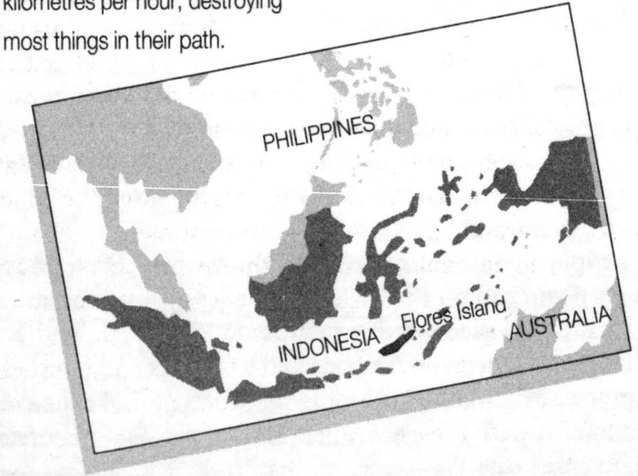

INDONESIA

Wall of Water!

It was noisy, the moment disaster struck. That was all Manha could remember afterwards. Noisy and confused, with nothing where it should have been. Suddenly his world had turned upside down in the most terrifying way.

The twelfth of December 1992 had started like any ordinary day. Well, not quite so ordinary for Manha, for he awoke in a friend's house in the city of Maumere, thirty kilometres south across the sea from his home on Babi Island.

Only 1300 people, including Manha's wife and four children, lived on tiny Babi. Manha had his own little wooden fishing boat. Every so often he would sail over to the much larger Flores Island where he would stock up with anything which the Babi-ites could not grow or catch for themselves.

The day before, Manha had waved goodbye to his wife who was busy tending the vegetables in their garden. His two youngest children, a boy, Donatus, and a girl, Christina, were helping her. He could see the sun shining on their beautiful black hair as they hoed away the weeds. His older son, La and daughter, Emilia, had already said goodbye and set about their chores around the back of the house somewhere. Manha thought that he could see some smoke from a fire. That would be Emilia, curing fish, so that it stayed good to eat, despite the hot sun.

Manha enjoyed crossing the sea to Flores, especially when he sailed alongside a school of dolphins, which were splashing and leaping in the clear water. After he had sold his latest catch of fish at a good price to the people who ran the cold store in Maumere, he had plenty of time to swap news with his friend before bedtime.

On that fateful morning of the twelfth of December he rose early and headed down to the colourful market district of the town. He soon found everything he needed, so he carried his purchases to the busy port, where his boat was moored.

Having stowed everything neatly, he returned to the market and spent a happy hour browsing again, trying not to buy too many 'bargains'. But he could not resist a bright red bouncing ball for little Christina. How she would love it!

There was no need to set off for home straight away, so, putting the tiny ball into his pocket, he took a walk around the city. He always found something to fascinate him there. For example, now he examined the street lamps. Not much by daylight, perhaps – but he himself had seen them lit up with electricity last night, something he saw only over here! People had to rely on firelight on Babi – or on little lamps. The kerosene needed to fuel them had been one reason for his shopping trip, earlier.

In Maumere the concrete buildings intrigued Manha – especially the bigger ones – churches, shops and the district office. Even some of the houses there reached high up into the sky, with one room perched on top of another, in a way which always seemed very strange to him. In Babi they made houses of wood or palm leaves – whatever they could find on the island. These sat on wooden stilts and the family's animals lived underneath. But no way could they have balanced one room over another.

By mid-morning, Manha was heading back to his boat. Though small, it had good sails and had always served him well. He had brought that boat home time and time again, full of tuna and scad and all sorts of other sea creatures for the family to eat.

Now he swung himself down off the jetty, untied the rope and gave himself a push off. He would be glad to be out where he could feel the sea breeze. Though it was not yet mid-morning, the sun beat down powerfully and he had to wipe the sweat from his face and hands.

Once out of the harbour he settled down. In times like these, when he was not busy fishing, he loved to look down through the clear waters to see if he could find some of the 'gardens of the sea'. Delicate corals stretched out their branches in these 'gardens'. Shining fish, in stripes of vivid colours, slid into view and away again.

When the water grew too deep for him to see the coral, he gazed at the palm-fringed beaches of the coast, where waters lapped in ever paler shades of turquoise at the edge of the white sand.

But Manha had only sailed a few kilometres when he realised that he had forgotten something important. Water. He had made it a rule never to set off without fresh water if his route lay across the sea, away from land.

No point now in sailing back to Maumere harbour. Plenty of streams ran down to the coast of Flores Island and he headed for a likely looking valley. Trees grew too thickly for him to see a stream, but still he sailed as close as he dared, then threw out the anchor and swam for shore, clutching his water-carrier.

Yes, there was the river. He could see a pool where it sank into the sand half way across the beach. Only it must have flowed over muddy soil, because its water looked brown and cloudy. Never mind, hills rose not far inland and Manha thought that he could hear a little waterfall. It will taste sweeter there, he thought.

He had to clamber up a sharp little rise before he found the water clear and fresh. As he straightened after filling his container, he heard a low noise, like distant thunder, or a heavy lorry passing down a narrow street in Maumere. Then, beneath his feet, he felt the earth shake.

An earthquake! He flung himself to the ground for the few seconds it lasted, praying that no tree would fall on top of him. And then he heard another noise, faint at first but growing loud enough to deafen him. Whatever could it be? It seemed to come from the direction of the sea. He peered down through a gap in the trees and the strangest sight which he had ever seen met his eyes.

There was his boat, still anchored, but the sea had gone! The boat lay on the dry ocean bed. No way could the tide have gone out that fast, Manha reasoned. Anyway, it looked all wrong. The water never left coral high and dry like that. And he could see a large fish, probably a tuna, flapping about near the boat.

The strange rumbling noise, which had receded, returned until it became so deafening that he had to cover his ears. And then he saw a huge wall of water rushing over the dry sea bed towards his boat. High as a palm tree, it was, and approaching fast as an aeroplane. Smooth at the top, not breaking like an ordinary wave, it carried branches and rubbish along with it – and something which must have been part of a fishing boat.

The wave had reached Manha's boat now, and tossed it out of sight as though it had been a fragment of leaf. Manha had no time to worry about his boat, for the water had reached the beach and was coming straight for him.

He clung to the trunk of a tree while it plunged over his head. How he lived through that impact, he never knew. He was later to find out that, wherever the wave hit the coast, some people had survived, though many perished. Up near the waterfall he had been higher than most.

Soon after it hit him, the water began to run back to the sea again, only to be followed a few minutes later by another wave. This time it did not quite reach Manha, who still clung, terrified, to his tree.

Minutes passed, or maybe hours – Manha had no real idea of the time. The sea seemed calm again, though the woods were a mass of splintered debris. On the side of the valley he could see a big hole where the earth seemed to have split apart.

He made his way down the slope, now slippery with mud. Then he found that the huge waves had pushed the beach about 400 metres inland. The smooth, white sand was littered with sharp pieces of coral and stone, torn up from the sea bed. He had to walk very carefully, to avoid cutting his feet.

Slowly Manha began to pick his way down towards the place where his boat had been. He wanted desperately to reach his family on Babi Island but he had no real idea of how he would get there.

And then he saw his boat, wedged up against a large bush. Somehow, it had survived, scratched and battered on the surface, but, so far as he could tell, otherwise whole. In a daze, Manha gathered some fat, round branches and used them as rollers under the boat. They helped him push it along until it floated in the water again.

He checked for leaks, but all seemed dry, so he hoisted the sail and set a course for Babi.

It seemed hours before he could see the island clearly. Manha knew the direction from which the *tsunamis* came and realised that they would have hit Babi before they reached him on the coast of Flores. He longed for news of his family, yet dreaded it at the same time.

As he came closer he searched with his eyes, but everywhere the island looked a wreck. He strained his ears, but heard only the sounds of wind and waves. He shouted like a madman, then, but no one replied.

Soon afterwards he saw the body of a man floating face down in the water, and then another. He was beginning to think that no one on the island had survived when he saw a third body. This one was moving, trying to attract his attention, shouting, 'Help!'

But Manha was past playing the rescuer. His only thoughts were of how he might find his wife and children. People were swimming towards him now and climbing aboard his boat. It rocked violently and began to take in water. Too many people would sink the little boat and then they might all drown. Manha tried to push the people away.

He was not going to die before he had found his family!

Shaking, Manha steered straight for the nearest bit of shore. Suddenly the boat stopped. It seemed to be caught up in something. Manha looked overboard and could hardly believe his eyes. It was caught all right, in the top of a palm tree, which seemed to be growing at the bottom of the sea. This must have been land, yesterday, he reasoned, trying to remember how things had looked just here. But, with so many things out of place, he could not get his bearings.

All this time he and the others were frantically pushing with anything they could find, trying to free the boat from the tree's clutches. Finally, they succeeded. They had nearly reached shore now. No longer caring about his precious boat, Manha leapt overboard and ran along the beach in the direction of his house.

All along the way he found dead animals and dead people. Flies were crawling over both, and the smell which filled his lungs made him choke. He knew every one of those people, but by now he was almost mad with grief and could think about nothing but his own wife and children.

When he came to the place where his house had been he hardly recognised it. Nothing was left standing, not even the huge coconut trees which his grandfather had boasted of climbing as a boy. The garden, where once his wife had grown many good things to eat, had become a mess of sand and rubbish.

Manha sank to the ground then, and cried in great sobs. He wept for his friends, but most of all for his family – for his wife and four children who had all been taken away from him. Perhaps if he had been here he could have done something, he thought. Or, more likely, he would have perished with them. Surely that would have been better than living without them! Oh God, how could this happen to him – to all of them on Babi Island?

Dark had fallen by the time a neighbour found him there, on the ground, his body still shaking. Silently she handed him a drink of water. Then she said something which made his heart beat faster.

'You know, a boat came, and took some of the people. Tomorrow you must look for your family on Flores Island.'

'What?' Manha did not understand.

'The boat will fetch the rest of us tomorrow. They have put tents there for us to live in and they will give us food to eat.'

'Are my people alive then?' he whispered, hardly daring to hope.

'I have not seen them, my friend, but it is possible.'

Though he felt incredibly tired, Manha found it impossible to sleep that night. He could do very little in the darkness, except pace up and down, thinking and worrying. In the end he sank to the ground, exhausted. He must have dozed, for the next thing he knew, his neighbour was waking him. He could hear the sound of a motor boat approaching. Twenty or so ragged survivors of the *tsunamis* were wading out through the shallow sea towards it.

Once everyone had climbed aboard, the boat sped off towards Flores. It could not go fast enough for Manha. He had to know whether his family had lived or died.

They arrived, not at Maumere, for that too had suffered terrible damage from the *tsunamis*. They did not even land at one of the coastal villages. The many small after-shocks of the earthquake threatened to topple even those few houses which remained standing, and no one dared go inside a building there.

They landed at a camp, sixty kilometres along the coast from Maumere. There, makeshift tents housed the refugees from Babi and two other small islands – Pamana and Besar. Food was being organised, they were told – and medicines should arrive soon. Many of the people had wounds which needed, at the very least, bandages and disinfectant.

Manha did not care about those things. He only wanted to find his family. He ran out of the boat, past the officials who wanted to take everyone's names. Manha was shouting his wife's name, and those of his children.

Frantically, he peered at people's faces, but recognised no one. Then at last he saw two boys from Babi Island. They ran up to him.

'Manha!' they exclaimed. 'You're alive! Your wife is here, and your daughter, Emilia!'

Manha just stared at them, but someone had gone to fetch his wife.

Tears streamed down both their faces as they met and embraced. Emilia followed on behind.

After he had hugged her too, Manha asked, 'And the others? What happened?' He had to know, though he dreaded what the answer would be.

Emilia answered, 'First the earthquake shook us and then the sea turned dry as land. Then it suddenly leapt up in a wave twenty-five metres high, or so they said. I saw it, taller than the coconut palms!'

Manha's wife took up the story. 'The wave seemed determined to devour our island. In a second the water rushed in. It moved the earth and smashed everything. And then another wave came, higher than the first. We all ran for our lives – but in an instant it had reached five hundred metres from the beach. It even caught people who had managed to climb a little way up the hill.'

'The land split and swallowed grown men, or so they said,' Emilia added, 'and water spouted, high into the air, out of new springs.'

'Afterwards they found our two boys – dead. The house had fallen on top of La – we think he was trying to rescue his brother, but it wouldn't have been any good.' Manha's wife paused and drew a deep breath. 'You know the metal roof of our house? The wave spun it off. Donatus got in the way. Its edge cut him in two, like a knife.'

Manha could hardly take it in, but his wife continued, in a flat tone, 'Christina is still missing.' Her voice shook now.

'Your boat brought the last of the survivors here, so I can only think that she too must be dead. Men from the navy are burying the bodies on Babi now. Four hundred, all in one grave.'

Gently she led her husband back to the tent which had been given to them. They had nothing else. No proper home, no money or way of earning it, no pigs or chickens, no clothes but the ones they were wearing. They lacked even the kerosene for a lamp – that had been flung out of the boat by the *tsunami*. December was the month for sowing seed in those parts, but no one had any now. All had been lost. And three of their family's four children had perished also.

As he bent to enter the tent, Manha felt a lump in his pocket. The little, red, bouncy ball, bought in Maumere market just the day before, had somehow survived the disaster which had destroyed so much.

'It was for Christina!' he sobbed.

That night, the three of them clung together in the little, makeshift tent. Manha tried to put on a brave face.

'We must be grateful for the help which we have received,' he said. 'For shelter from the rain and for food to eat.' By now they all knew that the north coast of that part of Flores had been hit almost as badly as Babi itself. Most buildings in Maumere city had become piles of rubble. No one could use the damaged harbour, nor any of the roads along the coast. Yet people from the local Catholic church had managed, somehow, to provide for the Babi-ites at the camp, and they were thankful.

'Somehow, we three are still alive,' continued Manha, continuing to think of the good side of their situation. 'And, most important, we have each other. We must help one another be strong. For only then, somehow, some day, we will build a new life for ourselves!'

BOLIVIA

- Bolivia is probably the poorest country in South America.

- Most people live by growing their own food and very few outside the main towns have safe water to drink.

- The Altiplano, a flatter area up in the Andes mountains of Bolivia, is nearly four kilometres above the level of the sea. It is cold there all the year round, and quite dry too. The soil is thin and poor.

- People who come up to the Altiplano from elsewhere have to take it easy for the first few days or they will feel ill, because the thin air at that height contains less oxygen.

- Tear Fund supports 25,000 children all over the world and 1,677 in Bolivia. They work with an American partner, Compassion, to provide food, school equipment and other support for poor children in many countries around the world. Christians in richer countries can help support a child, giving a certain amount of money each month, praying for and writing to them. (See pages 95-96 for details.)

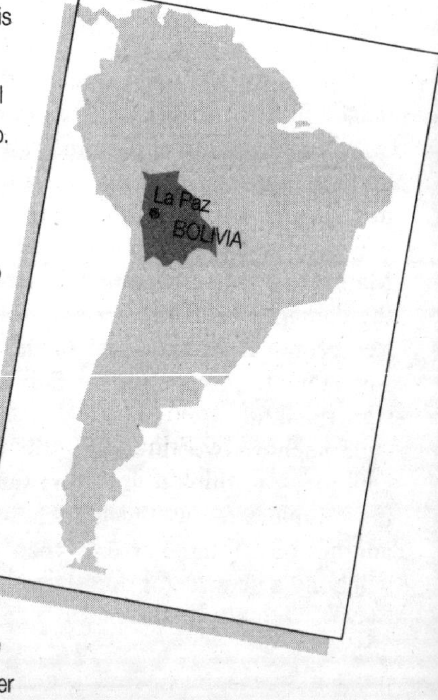

BOLIVIA

Writing to a Stranger

Dear Maria,
Mum says that we can write to you. I am Heather and I am eleven years old. My brother is called Simon and he is ten.

Heather looked closely at Maria's photograph again. With her pale brown skin, plump red cheeks and slightly slanting, black eyes, she looked like no one that Heather had ever met in England. She would have given anything for Maria's thick black hair, which she wore parted in the middle in two thick plaits.

Heather thought for a moment, pushing her own rather straggly brown hair out of the way, and then continued writing.

We like your picture. Can you tell us more about your family and about what you do in Bolivia?
With love from
Simon and Heather Davies.

'Yes, that's good, Heather,' said her mother. 'Can you copy it up neatly? Printing would be best.'

'But how will Maria understand what I've written? She speaks Spanish, doesn't she?'

Her mother nodded. 'You know how her letters come with her writing in Spanish, and then underneath someone has translated it into English?'

'Yes.'

'Well, someone in Bolivia translates our English writing into Spanish for Maria to read. If you leave an empty line under every line which you write, they will put the translation there.'

'Where is Bolivia?' Simon asked.

'I'll show you.' Mum lifted down the big atlas. 'First, let's find South America,' she said, leafing through the pages.

'Bolivia's got no sea!' Simon said, when Mum pointed out the country.

'That's right. And can you see this bit which is coloured purple?'

'Yes.'

'That means very, very high mountains. Look, there's the highest lake in the world, the highest lake you can sail round in a decent sized boat, anyway,' said Mum.

Heather peered at the page and read, 'Lake Titicaca. What a funny name!' she said.

'Is Bolivia a poor country?' asked Simon.

'Very poor, I think,' replied his mother. 'That's why Tear Fund helps support children there. We send them a certain amount of money every month and they pass it on to an organisation called Compassion, which runs schemes to help support children like Maria. They make sure she's got enough clothes and books and things to go to school – and enough to eat. And they translate the letters, of course.'

'I have to do a topic on a poor country this term,' said Simon. 'Mrs Hill has just told us. We only have three weeks and loads of people have chosen India. That's what I wanted to do, but she said that no one else can.'

'Well, why not do Bolivia, then?' said Mum. 'Let's see what we can find out.'

'What does Maria say in her letter?' Simon tried to snatch it off his sister.

'Now, Simon!' warned his mother. 'I have a whole pile of her letters, somewhere. We've supported Maria for about four years now and she writes about three times a year. Oh yes, here we are!'

'I greet you in the name of our Lord Jesus Christ,' Simon read.

He glanced over Heather's shoulder. 'You haven't put in any of that stuff, have you?' he said. Then, accusingly, 'You should have asked her more about Bolivia for my topic and you've gone and used up all the space, you stupid...'

'We'd never get an answer back in time, Simon,' his mother interrupted hastily. 'Bolivia's on the other side of the world – and don't forget all those translations which need to be done!'

Simon went back to reading Maria's letters. *I pray for you each day that God will bless you and your family.* 'Do you and Dad pray for Maria every day, Mum?'

'Well, no!' Mum looked slightly embarrassed. 'But we do pray for her sometimes, especially when we get her letters. And now perhaps you and Heather will pray for her as well.'

'Hmm.' Simon pulled a face and went back to reading Maria's letter.

I work hard at school. I have my exams soon. I help in the fields and I go to church every week. Thank you for your Christmas present. I bought a sweater.

'Christmas present? But it's June! When did this letter come?'

'A week or so back, Simon. Yes, it does take a long time for things to get through. We sent some money off last October, I think.'

Simon carried on reading the letter.

I pray that God cares for you. Your loving daughter in Christ, Maria.

Simon stared at the piece of paper in disbelief. 'Hmm,' he repeated, 'A topic on Bolivia's no way a good idea.'

'Why not, Simon?' his mother asked.

'Well, all they seem to do there is pray a lot and work hard. I mean, it's not very interesting, is it?'

His mother laughed. 'I think she is taught to be a bit more correct and formal when she writes letters than we would be. But you could find out more – go to the library and things. I'm pretty sure they play football there for a start.'

Simon cheered up for a moment. Then he pulled a face again. 'Not girls, though,' he said, gloomily.

But Mum was already digging deeper into the file of letters. 'Look, here's the sheet they sent us about Bolivia, Simon. That'll be useful.'

She handed Simon a sheet printed on both sides. The first thing he noticed was another map. 'So where does Maria live?' he asked.

'Near La Paz. Do you know, it's the highest capital city in the world? And Maria's up there in the high mountains, in a village somewhere.'

Simon was already reading the sheet. 'They have jungle in Bolivia too – jaguars and parakeets and things – why can't she live there?'

Mum laughed. 'Yes, that's part of the Amazon rain forest, I think, in another part of Bolivia. You could find out about that too. I don't think that very much grows where Maria lives, but they have llamas and things, and huge condor birds and ... and guinea pigs, I think.'

'Fiona in my class has a guinea pig,' interrupted Heather. 'He's so *sweeeet*! Can we have one, Mum?'

'Oh, Heather! When we had Harry the hamster, you never looked after him properly, did you?'

The next day, Saturday, Mum dragged Simon off to the shops with her, saying, 'You need a new school bag, anyway. The state of that one! I don't know *what* you do to it!'

'Do I *have* to come?'

'Yes, Simon, you do! And we can go to the big Central Library. It's no point looking for books about Bolivia in the little one down the road.'

No matter how much Simon protested, Mum insisted. It wasn't fair. Heather got to stay behind with Dad – and he'd probably let her spend all morning watching television! If only he'd put his hand up quicker for India, but then Mum said that all the library books on popular countries like that would have disappeared about ten minutes after school on Friday.

In the library, Simon asked a lady sitting behind the desk where he might find books on Bolivia.

'Over there,' she pointed, 'number 984.'

The librarian might at least have seemed impressed, thought Simon, trying to look as though he was the kind of boy who made regular expeditions to the jungles and mountains of far-off countries.

They flicked through the two books they found on the shelf.

'Might as well take both,' Mum said.

At least they had pictures in, Simon thought. He was surprised at the colourful clothes the people wore, especially the women, with their bright, full skirts and their shawls woven in vivid stripes. He had imagined that Maria would wear something much more dull. Yet the caption underneath the picture said that these women came from the area in which she lived – La Paz.

Mum smiled. 'The things those women are wearing on their heads are shaped just like bowler hats. When I was your age no businessman would have travelled into London without one!' Her eyes scanned the text.

'I don't believe it! This says that they copied the hats from British men who came to work on Bolivia's railways, years ago!' Mum exclaimed. 'You'll have to write about that, Simon!'

'Well, what exactly does Mrs Hill want you to do for your topic?' Mum asked when she had settled down back at home with a cup of coffee.

Simon was busy showing off his new 'army camouflage' school bag to Heather and did not answer at first.

Then he said, 'We have to find out why it's poor, I think. And the kind of houses people live in – all that stuff.'

'Haven't you got a Task Sheet?'

'Left it at school,' he grinned.

'Simon, you're hopeless! You'll be given detentions if you mess up doing homework when you get to secondary school!' Heather warned him.

Simon stuck his tongue out at her, behind their mother's back.

But Mum was leafing through the books again. 'I'm sure we can get you started, anyway, Simon,' she said. 'Look, here's a bit about houses.'

Simon read how many of the poorer people lived in one-room houses made of *adobe*, or mud and straw, with roofs of grass or reeds, no windows and no electricity or running water. He tried to imagine what that would be like, but soon gave up.

'Why *is* it poor?' Heather asked Mum.

'Well, not many people live there,' said Mum, stopping to think for a minute. 'And it must be hard to move things around the country with all those mountains. But then, I'm not quite sure, because they have lots of things like tin and oil which they can sell.'

She was looking through the other book now. 'One thing – they owe lots of money to other countries and a large part of what they earn goes to pay off the bank interest on that. If a country starts off poor, they need to borrow money to build roads or factories, and it's really hard for them to pay it back.'

When he went back to school that Monday, Simon found his Task Sheet and started writing up his topic. He had to do a chapter on schools in his chosen country. He knew that Maria went to school. She *liked* it!

'Children often do, in poor countries,' Mrs Hill explained. 'If your Maria works really hard at her lessons and then trains to be a nurse or something, that's probably the only way life is going to get any better for her or her family.'

Back at home that night, Simon looked up about schools in Bolivia. 'Over half the people can't read or write, but the government is trying to change that,' it said. 'The law says that all children have to go to school, but some children still don't because they live too far away from a school, or because their families need them to work, or because they can't afford the books and uniforms.'

'That's where Tear Fund's support scheme helps, I suppose,' Mum said.

'Do they have to stay at school till they're sixteen?' asked Heather.

'It says here that most Bolivian children don't go on to secondary school at all,' Mum pointed out. 'And it must be really hard for the little ones who are just starting. All the lessons are in Spanish, which most of them never speak at home. Imagine having all your lessons in French!'

Heather looked horrified. 'Maria speaks Spanish, though!'

'I think you'll find that she learnt it at school!' Mum corrected Heather. 'You should ask her next time you write. She and her parents must speak Aymara, or one of the other Indian languages, I reckon – she looks Indian.'

'But we're not doing India!' Simon looked puzzled.

'Sorry, Simon,' his mother laughed. 'Have you heard of the Incas and other people who used to live in South America before the Spanish came to conquer them? Well, they're known as American Indians – confusing, isn't it?'

'What, like Red Indians in cowboy films?'

'Kind of, but that's in North America,' Mum sounded a little distracted because she was hunting through the pile of Maria's letters for more information. 'It says here that she walks for an hour to get to school and an hour back at night!'

'An hour! Maybe Heather and me *had* better pray for her!'

'Two days a week she goes after school for a meal at the Family Centre which their local church runs. Oh, and look, they have a library there to help with the children's homework.'

'Big deal!' said Simon.

His mother ignored him. 'If she doesn't go to the centre

she has to cook the meal for the whole family, because her parents are still working. And then she has to start on her homework!'

'Where do her parents work?'

'In the fields. I've read all her letters through again and several of them say that their crops have failed. That must make things incredibly hard for them!'

Simon had become more interested in Bolivia now. He wrote about Maria in his topic book and Mum said that he could stick the picture of her in it.

He had worked hard. Mrs Hill was pleased. In Assembly he was given a 'Special Mention' for his topic, and five house points.

The next time Maria wrote, Simon grabbed the letter.

'My turn to write back this time,' he said. 'I know all about Bolivia now!'

I did a topic on your country, Simon wrote. *And I got good marks for it.*

'There, that's the school bit. Shall I say we're praying for her?'

'Are you?' asked Mum.

'Sometimes,' admitted Simon.

'Well, OK then, say we're all praying for her.'

After the long 'greetings' part of her letter, Maria had written about her three brothers and two sisters. Then she added, *I beg you to send to me a photograph of your family in England.*

Simon staged a raid on the odds and ends cupboard, sending its contents flying all over the lounge, before he found the latest packet of colour prints.

He pulled out one of them all on holiday, in swimming gear.

'You can't send that!' said Mum.

'Why not?'

'I don't suppose they go around like dressed like that in the mountains of Bolivia. Maria might be shocked!'

Next came a good shot of them in front of their house. 'That might make her feel, well, different,' Mum worried.

Finally they decided on a close up picture of Simon and Heather, standing together and smiling for the camera.

'Trouble is, it makes us look as though we like each other,' objected Simon.

'Well, you do, don't you – just occasionally?' teased Mum.

'At least *she* doesn't have to cook our dinner. Maria's brothers are well unlucky!'

'And you two are very lucky indeed!'

'Mmm.' Unusually, Simon turned quiet for a moment. Then he said, 'Mum, couldn't we help support someone else as well as Maria? A boy this time?'

'Not a bad idea, Simon,' said his mother. 'We'll all have to have a talk about that!'

INDIA

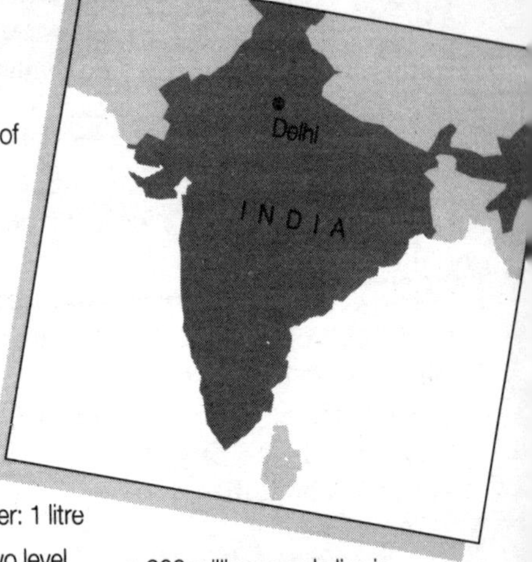

• Dirty water is the cause of eight out of every ten illnesses in the world.

• Nearly ten thousand children under five years old die of diarrhoea each week. If their parents gave them this recipe, most would recover: 1 litre clean water mixed with two level tablespoons of sugar or honey, plus half a teaspoon of salt.

• More people die each day from diarrhoea caused by dirty water than from all three of the things we think of as big killers – AIDS, cancer and heart disease.

• About nine million people in the world's poor countries have TB, an infectious disease which usually affects the lungs. 8,220 of them die each day, because they cannot afford the medicine which would make them better. Cheap injections would stop them catching TB in the first place.

• 900 million people live in India – more than any other country except China. In fact, one in every six people in the world is Indian.

• Twelve million people live in Delhi – over six times as many as in 1951. Three million of them live in slums.

INDIA

Death in the City

Geeta could not sleep. Her mother had been coughing for some hours now and, anyway, little Arun kept needing her. He had already called her six times that night. She had to half carry him outside. His thin legs would no longer support his weight because diarrhoea had made him so weak. Geeta worried because the skin beneath his eyes looked dark and shrivelled, while his body felt dry and hot.

The baby also kept crying. It seemed that only Father was sleeping – snoring in the corner. Had too much to drink as usual, thought Geeta, but she worried more about her mother and about her little brother, Arun.

She had tried, yet again, to talk to Father the day before. 'They have both been ill for too long!' she had sighed, a deep frown making her face look even more bony than usual.

But Father had brushed her aside, crossly. 'Don't talk to me now, my head aches like it will burst. I can't think about other people's problems!'

When could she talk to him, then, she wondered? If he wasn't drunk, he had a headache. Either way, he no longer seemed to care about looking after his family. But she said nothing. What was the use?

Mother's cough left her so weak that sometimes she hardly seemed to know what Geeta was saying to her. She realised that it was down to her, Geeta – the oldest of the children. I'll just have to manage, she thought. After all, I am ten now!

There had been two more in the family, but they had both died. So far as she could remember they had both been sick, just like Arun was now, running out into the alleyway because they had diarrhoea, until they could run no longer.

Geeta lay awake that night, wondering what on earth she should do. Towards morning, rain started thundering down on the thin metal roof of their shack, which in the slums was called a 'jhuggi'. She hoped that its walls would hold this time and not collapse, as one had a couple of months ago.

She hated rainy mornings. The alleyway outside smelt bad enough when dry. Everyone dumped their rubbish there and used it as a toilet. So did animals. Rain turned it into a stinking, muddy mess which splashed over her sandals and up onto her legs and clothes.

Not only that, the water she had to carry back for the family always tasted more foul than usual after rain, even when she boiled and boiled it. Mother used to say that germs in the water made the children get sick. 'People should not have to drink dirty water. It's not even fit for animals!'

Mother longed for them to move, but at least they had some sort of roof over their heads, thought Geeta. They were lucky to have a place to live, even if it was in the slums of Delhi. Many people lived out in the streets and begged for money or food.

The long night passed slowly. As she lay on the thin mattress on the floor, suddenly Geeta felt cold, despite the hot, damp air all round her. Mother might die – and Arun and the baby too! Father seemed useless these days and, if he had no money for a bribe, the slum lord might make him leave. Then, almost certainly, she would be living on the streets too – and dying there, probably.

I have to do something, she thought fiercely. Mother *can't* die, I can't let her. Nor must Arun. But what could she do? Who would help a poor family in a Delhi slum? There were thousands – millions – like them.

By morning, Geeta had hardly slept and her head felt heavy. She picked her way up the alley towards the pipe to collect some water. She carried two buckets, so she had no hand free to hold her nose and block out the smell. It had stopped raining. Flies were buzzing around the animals and on the dung and then settling on the food which some families were already preparing out in the open air.

The queue for water seemed longer than ever. Worried thoughts kept chasing around in Geeta's head. She did not feel like talking to anyone and stood waiting in a kind of dream.

Suddenly she heard something which jerked her awake. Two women in the queue behind her were talking about a doctor! Her family needed a doctor, but she had never heard of so much as a nurse ever visiting the slum.

No one there could afford medical help. Doctors and nurses earned good money looking after the people who had nice houses in other parts of the city – people who could pay them well. And why not? They were very clever people and had spent years training.

But the two women seemed to be saying that a doctor really was working in another poor area like theirs, a couple of kilometres away. Geeta just about knew where it was, although she had never been there.

At that moment she came to the front of the queue and had to concentrate on filling her buckets. Then she carried them back down the slippery alleyway, each of them so heavy that she thought her arms would drop off.

Back at the jhuggi-shack she made up the cooking fire, even though its smoke started her mother coughing worse than ever. She had to boil the water. As it heated she tried her best to give everyone a wash, using cold water from the other bucket.

Geeta knew that she had to try to find the slum doctor, though she worried about leaving the family, for Father had already gone out somewhere. But if I don't do it now, I never will, she decided.

She made herself as tidy as she could, whispered something to her mother and set off. On the edge of the area she knew, the traffic zoomed by in all directions. Bicycles, carts and motor vehicles all swerved wildly to avoid bony cows which wandered down the road. Geeta took a deep breath and raced across, hoping that nothing would hit her.

She turned along the road which ran down the side of some flats. By now she could see another area which looked just like her own – a mass of makeshift shelters, full of people, animals and rubbish. Only it seemed far bigger. However would she find the doctor – if there was a doctor? She was beginning to doubt that it could possibly be true.

She started walking down one of the alleyways, but felt as though everyone was staring at her. She did not belong here and she knew no-one. Supposing the slum lord grew angry, or robbers grabbed her? She had nothing for them to steal, so they might hurt her.

She held her head up high and tried to look as though she had a right to be there. Then she noticed two women, both wearing identical pale blue saris. They seemed to keep them very clean, despite the mud, and one of them carried a big rectangular box with a cross marked on it. They looked kind, and Geeta noticed that many people smiled at them. She wondered who they were.

A little further on she glanced down an alleyway which turned off to the right. Two more women in the same pale blue saris were heading away from her – and, yes, one of them was carrying a box too!

Geeta squeezed and dodged and slithered as fast as she could down the narrow alleyway after them. She hardly knew why, except that she had seen no one like them near her own home. She had formed some vague idea that perhaps they might know about the doctor.

'Excuse me!' She had caught up with them now. Both of them turned and smiled. 'I have to help some sick people and ... is there a doctor?' Her words tumbled out any old how, as she panted for breath.

'Dr Patel is in another slum at this very moment,' said one of the women. 'But can we help? Where are these sick people?'

'Well, they're over there. Quite a long way – behind the

flats.' She pointed, suddenly full of hope. 'Is the doctor there?'

'No, I don't think she's been to that place yet,' said the woman. 'Do you live there? I don't recognise you and I know nearly everyone here.'

Geeta backed away. Was this trouble? But the woman was asking if she knew who they were. When Geeta shook her head she explained that her name was Saroj. She had always lived in this slum, but a few years previously the doctor had arranged for someone to train her, and other women like her, as community health workers. Now they could give simple medicines and teach the people how to prepare food and water in such a way that it became safe to eat or drink.

'Then can you help my family?' asked Geeta, telling them about her mother and Arun. The two women listened carefully.

'If your little brother keeps having runny diarrhoea like that, he will lose so much water that he will dry up. That would kill him,' explained Saroj. 'You must see that he has plenty of clean water to drink. We will show you how to mix this powder into it.'

The powder was made of a kind of sugar plus some salt. It was very simple but when mixed with the right amount of water it replaced things which the body had lost through diarrhoea.

'As for your mother,' continued Saroj, 'she will need to see the doctor. From what you say I think she may have an illness called TB – it's very common around here. Now, don't worry, Geeta, it can be cured.'

The health workers showed Geeta the way to a small building used for clinics, asking her to come back to see the doctor there the next day. They explained how Dr Patel had worked in a nice hospital, until she felt God wanted her to come to the slum people, who otherwise had no one to help them if they were sick.

'But why?' Geeta wanted to know.

'She told us that Jesus spent most of his time on earth helping poor people. We thought she was a little crazy.'

Geeta followed the Hindu religion, like most of the people who lived in that part of Delhi. They believed that, once they died, they would come back to earth as something or someone else. What that was depended on how good they had been last time. So if they were suffering now, there was no point trying to make things better because it was a punishment for being bad last time.

Saroj told Geeta that the doctor, an Indian who originally followed the Hindu religion, had become a Christian when she was at school. She believed that God wanted to help poor people, not punish them. When she asked the slum lord for permission to work, he had lent her a chair and a table. She had set them up outside his house and started treating people.

Then, one day, a man came by. He worked in an important position for the government. He himself had grown up in the slums and he was shocked to see a nice young lady doctor working in such a place. Yet the more he found out about Dr Patel the more excited he became. The things which she did made sense. The man asked the government to help her buy medicines for the poor people. And some Christians in richer countries also gave money.

'Now we can immunise children so they don't catch some of the serious illnesses which used to kill so many of them,' the health worker said. 'Or give vitamin A, which is very cheap, but it can stop some people going blind.'

Soon that slum became so much healthier that Dr Patel had time to start work in other areas.

'Perhaps she will come to the place where I live,' said Geeta.

'Perhaps she will,' smiled the lady in the pale blue sari. 'But in the meantime, I will show you how to mix up more of this powder. I think it will help your brother.'

By the time Dr Patel came to visit Geeta's mother in her

jhuggi-shack, Arun had become so fit and full of energy that it took all Geeta's time to look after him and the baby. The doctor gave Mother a long course of medicine which slowly began to make her grow stronger again.

Better still, Dr Patel chose new health workers from Geeta's slum and trained them. Later, Geeta's mother became one of them. But certain things remained a problem. It was hard to make the drinking water really clean. Without drains and toilets, germs multiplied.

The doctor had a plan for that too. She held a meeting for all the grown-ups. She could arrange for the government to lend them money cheaply, so that they could build proper houses which would not fall down in the wind and rain. That was hard enough to take in – no one ever lent money to the people of the slums, but somehow they knew that Dr Patel could see to it. They would have to work hard and raise half of the money themselves, she explained, but suddenly it all seemed possible.

She would put them in touch with the right people in the government who would help them to dig proper drains. They would lay water pipes deep enough so that germs on the surface did not reach them. They could also have toilets, maybe not one for each family, yet, but enough for a few families to share. The government people could also help them to make proper alleyways out of concrete instead of mud and to put in electric street lights so that they could see to walk around after dark. And they mustn't forget a clinic, of course.

At first the people thought that Dr Patel was mad, but then she offered to show some of them a slum where the people had done just those things. 'It's still called a slum, but you wouldn't recognise it!' she laughed.

By the time Geeta reached the age of fifteen, she lived with her family in one of the new-type houses. Her wedding was already planned and soon she would have children of her own. She knew that it would be hard work, but thanks to Dr

Patel and the others, her young family would stand a better chance than her own brothers and sisters had done.

FACTFILE

ROMANIA

• Present-day Romania is made up of three old countries. A number of Hungarians and Germans live there, as well as Romanians – and they all speak different languages.

• In the 1940s Romania became a Communist country and in 1965 a very strict ruler called Ceausescu took over. He did not want any one group of people ganging up against him, so he tried to mix groups up by bulldozing Hungarian villages, for example, and housing the people in badly-built flats in other towns.

• In December 1989 a revolution in Romania took power away from Ceausescu and the other Communists, but the country had been so poorly run for years that life for ordinary people is still very hard.

• Around 80,000 people live in a town called Medias. Just down the valley, the factories in Copsa Mica, one of the most polluted towns in Europe, turn the air black.

• Medias and Copsa Mica are in Transylvania – a part of Romania which used to belong to Hungary. It is a land of rolling hills and wide valleys, with lots of fields and woods and some mountains. Transylvania is most famous for Vlad the Impaler (otherwise known as Dracula) who was imprisoned in a tower in Medias in 1467, but there is much more to the region than 'vampires'!

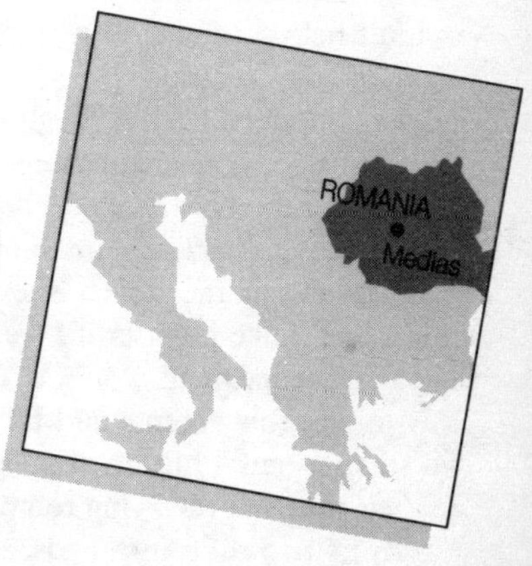

ROMANIA

High-Rise Tomatoes

Daniel clattered up the steps. The lift was still broken, but then he could hardly remember a time when it had worked. His little sister Elena kept grazing her knees on the rough concrete, but he was ten and he could run up and down the eight flights as quickly as anyone.

Inside the flat he dumped his school bag on the sofa which doubled as a bed at night.

'Pest – can't you keep the place tidy for two minutes?' his older sister Mihaela yelled at him, but he had dived into the bathroom.

'Hot water's off again!' she shouted after him.

Nothing in this place ever worked – half the time the electricity failed as well. Daniel splashed cold water on his face and hands, and wiped off the dirt with his towel. You couldn't help getting almost as dirty as a miner down a coal pit, after a day in Medias.

Daniel dodged back through the living room and ran out onto the balcony, where he aimed a kick at the railings. He hit them harder than he meant to, bruising his toe.

It's not fair, I can't do anything right, he thought. Mihaela never speaks to me unless she has something to grumble about. She'd like it better if I wasn't here. The others would have more space then!

As it was, his parents and the three children lived in just two small rooms – plus the tiny kitchen and bathroom. They ate their meals in the living room. Then every night they had to turn its two sofas into beds, which meant that you could hardly squeeze past the sideboard – the only other piece of furniture in the room besides the table. Next morning they had to pack the bedding away and turn the bedroom back into a living room again.

Daniel had just returned from a bad day at school. The others in his class had stayed on to play basketball in the yard, but they didn't want him. They said that he was too short and that he was rubbish at games. Even Bogdan, his so-called 'best friend', had told him to get lost.

No one likes me, he thought, as he stared gloomily out over the town. Nearby, other blocks of flats stood like grey slabs, casting black shadows in the strong sunlight. The day felt hot and sticky, but at least right up here a little breeze ruffled his hair. The air still smelt though – a familiar mix of the sickly pong from the town's tannery and sharper smells from the various chemical factories, which tickled the back of his throat.

The wind was not coming from the worst direction today. When it blew up the valley from the 'black town', Copsa Mica, they had to close all the windows in the flat, no matter how hot the weather, or they would all be coughing and retching. Sulphuric acid and carbon black did no one's lungs any good. Elena and his mother would be wheezing with their asthma and Mihaela would be in a worse temper than ever, for, however they tried to stop it, the sooty dirt crept into every room.

Daniel's gaze travelled further away, to the walls of the medieval city, with their sturdy towers. He loved to imagine himself back in those times, when knights were fighting the Turks and the grass grew green instead of grimy.

He clattered back through the flat.

'I'm going to the library,' he announced. Mihaela did not even look up until he was almost out of the door.

'You can get some bread from the market,' she said, rummaging around in a drawer and handing him a few coins. 'Here.'

'What's for dinner?' little Elena asked.

'Bread – unless you forget it like last time, Dan! And we've a little milk left.'

'Ugh – I wanted tomatoes,' moaned a high-pitched voice. Given the choice, Elena would have lived on nothing but tomatoes.

'Tough. That's the last of the money until Dad gets paid tomorrow – and bread will fill us up more than stupid tomatoes,' Mihaela snapped.

Daniel made a hasty exit to escape his little sister. She had become an expert at whining and was sure to put Mihaela in an even worse mood.

As he walked into town he tried to decide whether to buy the bread in the market on the way to the library, or to risk waiting until he came home again. He had no intention of hurrying back and he feared that, if he left it, all the bread might have gone.

In the end he stopped and bought a crusty loaf, tucking it under his arm. It smelt wonderful and his mouth began to water. Perhaps I could break off just a little bit without anyone noticing, he thought, but when he had done so, the loaf had an all-too-obvious hole at one side.

Bother! More trouble.

As he approached the library, he had an awful thought – would they ever let him in with his loaf of bread? He tried his most charming smile – the one he used at school when he had not done his maths homework. It rarely seemed to work with the teacher but now the library lady smiled back.

'Oh, it's you!' she said. 'After some more history books, are you?'

He nodded.

'Don't make crumbs, then!' She winked at him, and he understood that, if he kept the loaf pretty much out of sight, everything would be all right.

He spent the next couple of hours looking at pictures of armour and of castles and reading about the sometimes terrible things which went on inside them. He liked to imagine himself as a great and generous lord, routing his enemies and rallying his fighting troops. But he realised that, if he had been around in those times, more likely he would have been a peasant, toiling all day in the fields.

Even that had to beat working in factories, as his mum and dad did, he thought. Sometimes, in the summer, the Sunday School at his church took them all up into the hills and they played brilliant games in the woods and hay meadows. Up there, the air smelt clean and flowers grew and great birds flew about and he could run and run across great open spaces. He wished he didn't have to live in this smelly old town, even if it did have a good library.

Suddenly he realised the time. Mum and Dad would be home from work by now and Mihaela would kill him. As the oldest, she did much of the work of the house. She had left school almost a year ago, but she could not find a job and Daniel knew better than to mention that fact to her.

'Everyone used to have work under the Communists!' she had shouted at Dad one day – and that made him really mad.

Daniel clattered up the concrete steps and tried to catch his breath so that he could sneak in quietly with his loaf of bread. But he need not have worried. All his family were on the balcony – and they didn't seem interested in dinner.

'Come and look at this, Dan!' his father called, moving aside. Now he could see the object which the rest of them were crowding around.

How strange. It looked a bit like a plastic dustbin, with sticking-out pieces all round the sides and a flat top. It was about thirty centimetres across and a metre high.

'What is it?' he asked at last.

'It's called a Vertigrow. It means we can have a garden right here on the balcony – and raise our own vegetables!'

'Tomatoes, tomatoes!' Elena was dancing around in excitement.

'Yes, tomato seedlings, see? Courgettes and aubergines as well!'

'But I don't understand!' said Daniel.

His father explained. 'See this bag of compost here – it's like soil and we fill up these little pockets all round and up and down the sides – see them? We plant one seedling in each and water them every day and we should get a bumper crop, right here on the balcony!'

'They say thirty kilos during the summer months! I wonder if I can bottle some, so that we can eat vegetables in the winter, too!' Mum's eyes were shining.

'But where has it come from?' Daniel asked.

'From the church. Some people in richer countries give money so that the church can buy these Vertigrows. One old man spends his days raising the seedlings.'

'Are you sure it's going to work, Dad?'

'Yes. I've talked to other families who have them. And don't forget that I come from a village, I do. We had our own garden...'

'With three hens and a goat, and fruit trees and cabbages,' chorused Mihaela, Elena, and Daniel together. 'We do know, Dad!'

'I don't think we'll be able to plant plum trees in the Vertigrow!' laughed Mum.

'Ah, those wonderful fruit trees!'

Just then, Daniel glanced down from the balcony and saw his friend Bogdan walking along the street below.

'Hey, Bogdan!' he shouted, as loud as he could. 'Come and look at this.' Then he remembered that he and Bogdan weren't friends any more. It was too late. A few moments later an out-of-breath boy was pounding on the front door.

'We've got a garden on our balcony!' Elena had seized Bogdan's hand and was dragging him through the living room.

'Don't believe you!'

'Believe what you like!' crowed Daniel. 'I'm going to help grow lots of vegetables and then we're going to eat them.'

'It's true, Bogdan,' Mum smiled.

After that Bogdan became nearly as keen as Daniel and the rest of the family to see what was happening to the garden on the balcony. It didn't seem to matter so much that Daniel was rubbish at sports now – he had something that not many people had. Other boys from the class came to visit the flat. Mihaela let them help water the plants after school. They grew so fast!

Elena could hardly wait for the tomatoes to ripen.

'No, you can't eat them green, you'll have tummy ache,' her mother warned. 'They'll taste all the sweeter for waiting!'

A few days later, more seedlings arrived and Dad said that Daniel and Bogdan could help plant them.

'Green peppers and cabbages this time!'

Daniel explained, 'Dad loves cabbages. I think he misses his village, because they had loads of them there.'

'I wish we had vegetables for free like this,' Bogdan sighed. 'My mum says there's hardly ever enough money to buy them.'

'Dad said that as you've helped, you can have some when they're ready,' said Daniel.

'Did you say they were from your church?' Bogdan sounded puzzled.

'Sort of – the church organises it, anyway.' The boys were firming the compost around the roots of the tiny seedlings which they had planted in the Vertigrow.

'What's this church of yours like, then?'

'It's great – loads of people go there – more and more each week, especially since the revolution. It's really squashed now in the services. People have to stand in the lobby outside and in the gaps between the seats – everywhere. When we go out to Sunday School the grown ups have more room.'

'You go to school on Sundays too?'

Daniel laughed. 'Not like that! We have stories – about missionaries and things – and ones from the Bible. They're exciting. And we play games and things. It's good.'

'My dad says he doesn't see the point of going to church!'

'Well, *my* Dad says – oh, come on, don't let's argue again, Bogdan!'

'Well, I s'pose at least the church has given you a garden,' Bogdan had to admit.

Dad had overheard. 'And, more important, it's given us some hope that things will begin to grow again – and I don't just mean vegetables!'

FACTFILE

UGANDA

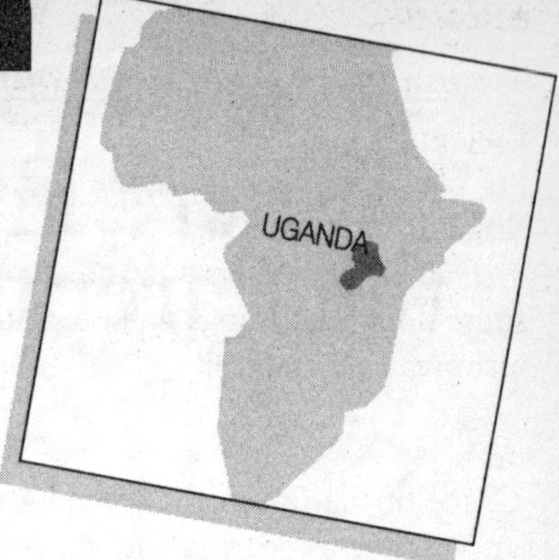

• Uganda, in East Africa, has a wonderful, warm climate, beautiful lakes and mountains and enough rain so that green plants grow everywhere. It should be a great place to live, but it has suffered more than its fair share of troubles.

• From 1971-1986 as many as two million Ugandans were killed in fighting, either between tribes or by order of the government and army of that time.

• One President of those times had all Asians thrown out of the country, but they had run most of the businesses and shops, so hardly anything worked any more.

• During the bad years, so much money went into fighting that there was not enough for hospitals. Soldiers destroyed people's farms so they did not have enough to eat. Illnesses like TB and measles wiped out millions more. If people had received proper care, these illnesses should not have killed them. Now AIDS is spreading in a big way.

• AIDS is caused by a virus – HIV – which destroys the body's ability to protect itself against infection.

• More than one in ten adults in Uganda are infected with HIV. That means more people will die of AIDS there within the next ten years than were killed in the fighting.

• Because so many adults have died, Uganda is full of orphans – and, because of AIDS, the problem can only get worse.

UGANDA

Where Have All the Parents Gone?

Grace lit the fire in the separate hut which was the kitchen, and started preparing the *matoke*. She peeled and chopped the green banana-like vegetables, then jammed the pieces into the pot of water which she had balanced carefully on stones over the flames.

Inside the other hut, Mother was coughing again. Grace muttered something under her breath. Not that she minded keeping an eye on Mother – but it seemed as though, whatever needed doing around here, Grace ended up doing it. Serve her brothers and sisters right if the food spoilt, she thought. Tiredness and worry had made her unusually spiteful.

Grace hurried to fetch a drink of water, but as she bent over the bed she noticed that blood stained the corner of her mother's mouth.

'Where's John?' Mother wheezed as she asked the question.

'Down by the river somewhere, I s'pose.'

Mother frowned. It seemed that, being the oldest of the children, Grace had to do so much these days. At two and four, Benjamin and John were too young to help much, but a strong ten year old like Silas could have done more than gather firewood – and that under protest. After all, Grace herself was only twelve and she had been working hard for years!

'And Patience?' Mother frowned again. Marjorie, who had just reached her seventh birthday, took her fair share of growing food in the garden, but Patience, though she was two years older, ran wild. Now that Mother was too ill to chase her, Patience had proved brilliant at escaping most of the chores, with a laugh and a 'disappearing' trick.

In truth, Mother worried about Grace, but Grace thought that Mother's frown meant that she was angry with her. She just shrugged and ran back to the kitchen again, muttering something about the pot boiling over. She hated to see her mother worried about the children. She felt guilty because, as the oldest, surely she should have been able to organise the others to work. Then they would not have time to get into mischief by the river, or on the swampy land.

But they never took much notice of anything *she* said, she thought, gloomily, as she stirred the *matoke*. And, in the end, it was easier to do the work herself.

Suddenly, Grace was aware of a small noise, right behind her. She spun round and her face changed as a big smile spread across it.

'Margaret! What you doing creeping up on me like that?'

Margaret was not only Grace's cousin, but her best friend. She and her six brothers and sisters lived with their (and Grace's) grandmother in the same village.

'Surprise, surprise!'

'Come on, you're hiding something behind your back!' Grace made a grab for it.

'No, careful!' Margaret laughed, holding out her two hands. One cradled three eggs, the other four.

'Old Solomon gave a whole load to Gran. We're all having one and these are for you!'

Old Solomon Mngedi kept more chickens than anyone else in the village and it seemed that they were laying especially well at the moment.

'When was the last time you tasted egg?' Grace's mouth was watering. Something different to go with the coarse yellow mush of matoke for once!

'This morning, of course! But how's Auntie today?' asked Margaret and Grace's face fell again.

'Like that, eh?'

Grace nodded. 'She hasn't got out of bed since Easter.'

Margaret hated to see her friend so miserable. 'Grandmother will always help look after you!'

'Grandmother is old. And she already has seven of you.'

Margaret's father had been killed at roughly the same time as Grace's. The two brothers had both joined Museveni's guerilla army when President Obote was still in power. They died fighting for control of an important town in the west of Uganda. Many perished before it was won.

Heroes, people called them. Certainly, now that Museveni and his people were in power, villagers were no longer carted away and killed by soldiers in the middle of the night. Even so, Grace secretly wished that her father and uncle had not gone to fight.

'What's the use of dead heroes?' she had asked Margaret, once, but Grandmother had overheard.

'Hush child,' she said.

Suddenly Grace felt guilty. She had hoped that, if anyone would understand and show her sympathy, Margaret would. A year or two after their fathers were killed, Margaret's mother had become weaker and weaker. Her skin developed sores and itchy patches. She suffered from diarrhoea and finally, at the end of a long and painful year, she died.

Grace now realised that Margaret had a special reason for not wanting to be reminded of that time. They called Margaret's mother's illness 'Slim' in Uganda, because people who caught it lost so much weight.

Grandmother said that she did not remember a single person becoming sick with it in her young days, but now she kept bemoaning how many they had lost to 'Slim', as well as to all those battles. It seemed that 'Slim' had come like some evil spirit and that no one, not even doctors in places like England and America, could stop it taking people away.

When Margaret's mother became so ill with 'Slim', people in the village turned against her. They said that she was under a curse and had refused to visit or speak to her.

When she died, Grandmother had taken in Margaret and her six brothers and sisters. Now Grace's mother had TB and Grace was very worried.

'Oh Margaret, how are we going to manage, with no one to earn any money?'

'You can grow *matoke* and *dodo*. I'll help. Plenty of people manage.'

Grace still looked doubtful and on the verge of tears.

Margaret put her hands on her hips and pretended to tell her friend off. 'Grace, cheer up, girl. Your face is as miserable as if old Solomon had stolen something instead of giving you eggs!'

'Sorry.'

'Come on, that *matoke* must be cooked by now. Why don't we call the others? I presume you're inviting me to lunch?'

After they had all eaten, Grace walked with Margaret to see Grandmother. They found her outside her house, scolding and chasing the little ones to clear up after their meal. While Margaret took over, Grace seized the chance to talk about her worries.

To her surprise, Grandmother took her seriously.

'Yes my dear. It is hard for you without a father and with your mother sick. And it is worse because so many have been taken from this village. I see it filling up with children who have no parents – not just from our family.'

'Eh...!' Grandmother clapped her wrinkled old hands together twice as she thought. 'For some time I have wondered if I should talk to the people in charge. Maybe even go to the Resistance Council.'

'Could you do that?' Grace asked. President Museveni had arranged that each group of four or five villages should elect people to serve on a Resistance Council to look after their local affairs. They seemed to work quite well.

Grandmother stopped frowning. She had made a decision.

'I could certainly talk to old Solomon. He is our representative on the Council, the one we grown-ups from this village chose to look after matters concerning our health.'

Things moved fast from then on. It turned out that the Resistance Council had already spent a great deal of time thinking about the problem. They had discussed the action to be taken with the District Health Officer. Margaret rushed over with the news a couple of weeks later.

She started talking about a church, but Grace did not really understand what this had to do with anything. Grace had certainly heard talk about a church which met in a clearing among trees near the next village. People walked from miles around to services held there.

'So what?' Grace asked.

'Well, Gran says that the church has already been talking to the Council about a clinic. They're hoping that this clinic will start coming round all the villages round here – including ours!'

'How?' Grace tried to imagine a building being pushed along.

'Nurses would bring everything they needed in a Land Rover.'

Grace began to see it now. Most villagers had no hope of finding transport to take them to see a nurse or doctor, so what a brilliant idea!

Grace found out more from Grandmother, who had learnt it all from Solomon. Apparently, nurses would be able to treat people who had certain illnesses. They would also try to help any they could not cure. They would send specially trained people to talk with them and help them to plan for the future of their children.

The clinic would also sell some medicines. Not give them away, or people might sell them again and keep the profit for themselves. But they would sell the medicines at a price which people could afford. Teachers would also come to help the people understand how to live more healthily.

'When are they coming?' Grace wanted to know. Everything happened so slowly around there. Would the clinic arrive too late for her mother?

'Solomon told me that the Resistance Council has already met with people from the mobile clinic many times. He thinks they will be given permission to start work soon.'

Sure enough, a week later the Resistance Council sent word that everyone was to gather that afternoon under the big tree in the middle of the village. The clinic would arrive and the whole village should greet them. Grace would not have missed it for anything.

It was all very correct that first time, with long speeches from the head of the Resistance Council. But then a young man from the clinic got up. He said that his name was Steven and he spoke well. He's probably been to college, Grace thought, enviously. He explained how the clinic worked and then he started to talk about 'Slim'.

AIDS, he called it. He explained that no one must be frightened of talking to a person who suffered from AIDS – you could not catch it that way. These AIDS patients needed plenty of people who would be willing to come near and help them if they were sick. He showed them charts with pictures on and explained the two main ways of catching the illness. The first was if the blood of someone who had it got mixed up with yours. But the second and most common way was if you had sex with them, even if they did not seem to be ill at the time.

'Be faithful. Only sleep with one person all your life,' Steven said, 'and if that other person only sleeps with you then "Slim" will leave you alone.'

After he had finished, people queued to see the nurse. Grace joined them. She herself felt fine, but how else could she get these people to help her mother?

When she reached the front, to her surprise the nurse promised that she would come that very day to visit Mother at home. Grace waited until the rest of the queue had been seen and then showed the nurse the way to her house.

The nurse, Angela, examined Grace's mother, and then spoke gently. She asked about the children, and gave a few pills to help the pain. Then she prayed, asking God to take care of all the family.

Outside, Angela spoke quietly to Grace. 'Your mother has TB – badly. There's not much we can do, except to make her a little more comfortable,' she said. 'But I believe that God will look after her, even if she dies.'

Grace was shocked. No one in the village ever mentioned that a person might die.

Angela could see how she felt and tried to explain. 'Yes, I do talk about dying, even though it is not our custom to do so while someone is still alive. But, if that person is very sick, it is best to face the possibility, to prepare for it, to think about what might happen to all of you who are left.' The smooth dark skin of her face creased into a frown. 'What about the house? Has your father a brother who might take it?'

That was something which had been secretly worrying Grace for some time. 'Yes, it is his right, although my uncle lives far away and ... I do not know what he will do.'

Angela's big dark eyes were so kind that they somehow gave comfort to Grace. 'You know, whatever happens, even if your mother does die, you should put your trust in God. I believe that he will look after you and your family.' She smiled. 'Courage, now. We will be back again soon!'

True to their word, the clinic did keep coming back and sometimes they brought other people who had nothing to do with medicine. One man showed the whole village ways of growing better crops on their land. This meant that those who wanted to help the orphans in the village, but who had been able to grow barely enough to feed their own families, now had food to spare.

It was not many weeks before Grace's mother died. Many people came to the funeral, staying for up to a week, sitting with the family, to comfort them. People whom Grace hardly knew wept and wept.

Angela, the nurse, said how sorry she was that her mother had been too ill for them to make her better. She called all the children in the family together and told them that their mother was right now as happy as could be, in heaven, with Jesus, with no more cough and no more pain.

She had become quite a friend by now. Grace knew that she could talk to Angela and that she would listen and help, either in practical ways or at least with an honest sensible reply. But today, even Nurse Angela's kind words did not comfort her much. Fine for Mother, not so fine for herself and the rest of the children!

When their uncle came and said that he wanted a talk with Grace, she became very worried. If he took their house, as was the custom in Uganda, what would become of them? She did not know him very well, since he had settled with his own family in a different part of the country. He had a kind face, though, she thought.

He questioned her closely at first, about how she had managed when Mother had been so sick. She explained about how they had grown their own food on the land around their house. She told him about the clinic and how people in the village had been especially kind since it had started its visits.

'So, child, if I leave you the house and return to my own family, will you be able to look after your young brothers and sisters?'

'Oh yes!' Grace's eyes shone. 'Grandmother is here to watch out for us too!' she added hastily.

'And all your friends from this village – and the clinic,' smiled Uncle. 'And most of all, I hear how hard you work. I think that the little ones will be in safe hands.'

The next time Grace lit the fire ready to prepare the *matoke*, she was surprised to find Patience and Silas at her side.

'Can we help?' Patience asked.

Grace grinned. Grandmother had disappeared with Uncle for a while before he left that morning. She had thought that Patience and Silas had run off to the river, as usual. But now she wondered if they had all had a 'little talk.'

'Can you peel these, if I cut them up?' she asked Patience. 'And someone needs to do some digging if we're going to plant the *dodo*,' she smiled at Silas. They were going to manage. She knew they would.

WHAT DOES TEAR FUND DO?

When Jesus began his work on earth, he said that God, his father, had chosen him, 'to bring good news to the poor.' He healed the sick, fed the hungry and forgave those who had done wrong.

As an evangelical Christian charity, Tear Fund tries to follow the example of Jesus. We believe in meeting the needs of the poorest people in the world by putting Christian love into action. We are actively involved in healing the sick, feeding the hungry and bringing new hope and lasting change to people in need.

Today Tear Fund is working in all of the countries you have read about in this book and in many others around the world. We work through local Christians who are trying to help poor people, whatever their beliefs, colour or race.

When disasters happen, like the story of the *tsunami* in Indonesia, Tear Fund helps local Christians to get things like blankets, tents, medicines and drinking water to those affected by the disaster. In the 1990s Tear Fund has already given millions of pounds to help people in disaster situations around the world.

But we don't just help people in disaster situations. We also help them work towards a better future. Children are really important to Jesus, whether from the city streets, as in the story from Brazil, or from the countryside. There are real places like Hope Village which Tear Fund helps to support. We also have a programme called Partners in Childcare through which people in this country help over 25,000 children in other countries. Through this programme, children get regular meals, clothing, education and healthcare.

Healthcare is really important – not just healing people when they are sick, but helping to prevent sickness. The story called 'Death in the City' is based on the ASHA project in India which began in one slum with a doctor called Kiran Martin. ASHA has grown and is now working in eleven slums in various parts of the city, training health workers who, like the ones in the story, are dressed in pale blue saris. Once again, Tear Fund is helping this project and many others like it.

Most of the diseases in the world are the result of dirty water supplies. 24,000 children die each day because their water supply is dirty, spreading diseases like cholera, typhoid or dysentery. Tear Fund are committed to helping people like those in Burkina Faso to have clean water.

One of the hardest health problems to tackle at the moment is AIDS. Many people are suffering and dying as a result of this disease and thousands of children have become orphans. Almost everyone in the country of Uganda seems to know someone who has died or is dying of AIDS, but the Ugandan Christians are doing a wonderful job in caring for the sick and teaching others how to avoid catching the virus.

In many countries like Sudan, Bosnia and Rwanda, where there are terrible wars, it is more difficult to help people on a long-term basis. But we are still able to work through Christians there and provide shelter, food and medicine for people who have often had to leave their homes, families and possessions behind.

When the environment is destroyed, as in the story set in Honduras, people's lives are at risk as well as God's beautiful creation. A lot of Tear Fund's work involves helping people to protect and renew their environment. This means helping, not just with land rights but with tree planting, soil protection, solar power, wind power and many other projects that help people take care of the earth.

If you would like to have more information about Tear Fund or to get one of our regular magazines for young people, free of charge, write to me at the address below.

Barbara Gallagher, Youth Communications Co-ordinator
Tear Fund, 100 Church Road, Teddington, Middlesex, TW11 8QE

If you want more information about supporting a child, write to **Carole Allen, Partnership Manager** at the same address.

Readers in Australia and New Zealand should contact the following:
TEAR Australia, PO Box 289, Hawthorn, VIC 3122
TEAR Fund New Zealand, PO Box 8315, Auckland